solace in seven

An erotic novella

k.l. hall

Solace in Seven: An Erotic Novella

K.L. Hall

synopsis

Fresh off a breakup and mending a broken heart, Cassidy Stokes has sworn off all men from now until the hereafter. Now as the only single gal on what was *supposed* to be a couples' getaway with her girlfriends and their men, she decides to use her time on the island of St. Martin to reconnect with herself. After all, self-love is the best love. What was supposed to be a week filled with an abundance of R&R, turns out to be the trip from hell when she's face-to-face with her high school foe, NBA superstar, Hendrix Croft.

With cognac brown eyes and caramel skin as smooth as satin, Hendrix "The Tomb Raider" Croft hasn't aged a bit. He's still sexy as sin and the bane of Cassidy's existence. While recovering from an injury, news of his trade to one of the worst teams in the league hits the airways, making him the subject of endless gossip. He elects to get away for a mental break from the palm trees and plastic groupies that come with having a multi-million dollar jump shot.

When a reservation error at a prominent resort lands them in each other's close company for seven days, they are forced to play nice or not at all. With a heart more jagged than cacti, what will Cassidy do when her misery starts to desire his company?

"Twenty something, all alone still.
Ain't got nothin', runnin' from love.
Only know fear.
That's me, Ms. twenty something."
-SZA

.

the prelude

Day Six

Cassidy Stokes

"You so fuckin' nasty, you know that?"

Hendrix's facial expression was set to a handsome scowl as he palmed the back of my head as if my last name was *Spalding.* He leaned his head back against the door as my lips slid up and down his dick. Nice and sloppy, just the way he liked it. What touched the back of my throat wasn't just any dick. He had a dick to rival everyone from my past. It was *definitely* something to write home to Mama about. I was supposed to be celebrating my cousin, Lauryn's engagement, but instead I teetered on the four-inch heels and the tips of my toes, trying my best not to let my knees touch the floor of the cramped restroom bathroom stall we occupied. *A men's bathroom stall at that.*

Unsanitary.
Unforgiving.
Un-fuckin-believable.

We'd crossed a line we never should've fuckin' crossed. Matter of fact, we'd done figure eights over it, but I was down to do whatever he wanted me to. I'd come to the island of St. Martin to get over my old nigga, not get under a new one—one that I couldn't stand at that, but Hendrix and I were far from the shallow end. To make it all make sense, let me start from the beginning...

one

. . .

Before the D.

CASSIDY

"If you could build the perfect nigga, what would be some of your must-haves?" my best friend, Lauryn, asked.

I pulled the phone away from my ear with a frown across my face. "Why are you asking me this?"

"Because I need you to get out of this funk you've been in!"

"I told you, I'm fine," I assured her.

"Have you tried dating apps? You know, to get your feet wet again."

"For what? To be bombarded with unauthorized dick pics from niggas who have pinky dicks in real life? No thanks."

"I had a nigga with a small dick once. You remember Carlos from Wayberry?"

"Yeah, I do."

"Girl, yikes. That shit was mega small, too. And all he ever wanted to do was eat my fuckin' pussy. I mean morning, noon, and night. Breakfast, lunch, and dinner, bitch. Believe it or not, it was really fuckin' annoying." She chuckled.

I chuckled before kissing my teeth. "Well, at least you got some reliable dick now. I, on the other hand, never want to see another dick again."

"Um, about that. You've been sending me all types of cryptic messages, cryptic signals, and cryptic vibes and shit when it comes to this breakup with Omar, and you need to spill the tea."

"What's there to spill, Lauryn? You asked what happened, and I told you."

"So, he just up and left? Just like that? With no explanation?" she quizzed.

"Nope," I lied.

Some things were better left unsaid. There was no way I was going to let Lauryn or the rest of my girls know the full story. He'd cheated on me with his ex over Thanksgiving break when he flew to Florida to be with his family. My company was launching a new product for Black Friday, so I had to stay behind in San Jose. Turns out, he'd had turkey for dinner and his ex for dessert, which resulted in her getting pregnant. I carried around enough shame and embarrassment, and I didn't need it from my girls. I was nobody's charity case or pity party.

"Wow, that's some fucked-up ass shit."

"Some bitch shit," I corrected her, my glacial voice holding a bitter note. "I *wish* I had a crystal ball to predict that shit."

As much as I tried to play it cool, the pain tore through my entire body like a raging wildfire. I raised a glass of Merlot to my lips while thinking back to the anniversary dinner date from hell that turned my heart into an emotional wasteland three weeks prior.

Omar sat across from me with his pecan brown eyes locked on his iPhone screen. It was easy for him to fade the buzz of the restaurant into the background, me included. I'd been trying my best to make pleasant conversation with him since we'd been seated, yet whatever was in his phone clearly had his full attention.

"Can you please put your phone down and talk to me?" I asked, glancing down at the half-eaten California roll we shared.

"It's work."

"Okay, and? You've been distant for months, and all I'm asking for is a couple hours of your time. I thought going out tonight would be special."

"What's so special about tonight? It's Thursday."

"Yeah, but it's the anniversary of our very first date, Omar. I've been working like crazy, and I know you have too. I thought we could use this alone time to rekindle the flame," I said, reaching across the table and grabbing his hand.

He slowly slid his hand from underneath mine and quickly sloshed the rest of his Moscow mule down the back of his throat. "There's something I need to talk to you about, Cass."

"Can it wait? I really just want to enjoy tonight, baby."

"No, it can't."

I straightened my posture, unsure of what was about to fly off his lips. "Okay. What is it?"

"I'm uh—I'm going to be a father."

My brows squinched together as my heartrate started to escalate. "Omar, what are you talking about?"

"I'm sorry, Cass. I'm so fuckin' sorry."

I looked across the table at the man I'd shared a life and my bed with, for the past eighteen months, in disbelief. There was so much I could say, yet nothing dare made it past my lips. I tried to wrap my head around how I could go from having a heart full of love for someone to hating them in a matter of seconds. When the words finally found their way off my tongue, out came an explosion of great proportions.

"Sorry for what, Omar? Tell me you're not serious!" He reached out for my hand, and I quickly snatched it away. "Tell me this is a joke!"

"I wish it was, but it's not."

"Who is she?" I asked, quickly stiffening my tone.

He lowered his head as his waves glistened under the soft ambient lighting. There was an aggrieved look across his honey brown face as if saying her name out loud would cause him pain. Omar parted his soft pink lips and mumbled, "Malaya."

My eyes bulged as if someone had clamped off my air supply. "Your ex, Malaya?"

Instead of responding with a yes or no answer, he simply nodded his head like an introverted schoolboy.

"She didn't tell me about the baby until February."

"Omar, it's about to be fucking May. Are you kidding me right now? You've known for months and you're just now getting around to telling me? And of all the times to find out, it would have to be on the anniversary of our first date. Wow, fuckin' classic, nigga," I said, giving him a round of applause.

"Cassidy, stop it before you cause a scene."

"Nigga, you are a scene! Are you listening to yourself? This is not a fuckin' BET movie. This is my life! You're fucking with my life!"

"Don't you think I know all of that, Cass? I've been fucked-up over this for months now, just trying to figure out what the fuck I was gonna do."

"Oh, so you were only fucked-up about having a baby, not the act that created the baby in the fuckin' first place? Keep talking, Omar. You're doing an amazing job," I said sarcastically.

He puffed out an aggravated sigh. "So, I'm telling you this because I—I've decided that I'm going to move back to Florida, t—to be there for my son."

I pressed my lips together tightly as I locked eyes on my untouched glass of water.

All I wanted was Omar out of my sight for the rest of my days. Love be damned, I never wanted to lay eyes on Omar Devante Greyson again! All the energy had been sucked out of my body to the point where I couldn't even yell at him like I wanted, no—needed to. "Son? It's a—it's a boy? Wow. Congratulations. Go ahead and order another round. This drink is on me," I said, before swiping up my glass and tossing the water right in his face.

I left him sitting in the restaurant, drenched and embarrassed as I ran back out to my car with makeup, smeared tears, and a runny ass nose like a toddler. The moment I got home, I put down roots in my bed and embedded myself in my depression for a full twelve days. I told my job there had been a death in the family, and they allowed me to work remotely when I could while I "grieved the loss of a loved one." Little did they know, I was just mourning over my heart that had been blown to smithereens.

"Cassidy? Cass? Hello? Cassidy Jhene Stokes, answer me!" Lauryn yelled, bringing me back to the present.

"Y—yeah, I'm here."

"You okay?"

I nodded as I hugged my knees to my chest. "It just hurts, that's all," I admitted, fighting back tears.

"Listen, I get it. But if he could just up and ghost you like that with no explanation then he just wasn't the nigga for you, which means there's someone else out there that's better."

"That's cool and all, but I don't want any man ever again."

"Bitch, who you tryna fool? You a Stokes girl like me, and we love the D!"

Knowing she was right, I let out a soft chuckle. "Whatever!"

She laughed. "I'm serious! Please snap out of it, sis. Depression is not a good look on you."

"I'm good. I told you that weeks ago."

"You're forgetting I actually know you, right? Like, we share the same blood. And I know you got your eating pants on right now don't you? Burn them shits, Cass, or I'll do it for you!" she warned.

"Whatever!"

"Don't 'whatever' me! I have not been bustin' my ass in the gym getting ready for a trip that you helped me plan for you to be fuckin' up all my pictures! Family or not, I will crop you out if your ass looks ugly!"

"Oh my God, you're so dramatic!"

"And? It's my birthday, and I need you there, Cass! Plus, you're my cousin and my best friend. I don't want you to feel like you have to go through things alone."

"I just don't want to be thinking about his ass the entire trip. Nor do I want to be the third fuckin' wheel with you, Brielle, Shauna, and y'all niggas."

"You won't! I promise we will all still hang out just us girls without the guys, but you still have to come to St. Martin!"

I rolled my eyes. "Swear on Big Mama's grave."

"Now you know you wrong for that."

"Do it."

"Fine, I swear. So, it's settled. You're going!"

I let out an exasperated sigh. "I'm going," I confirmed. "Come hell or high water, I'll be there with my vibrator in tow."

It wasn't like I had much of a choice. Depressed or not, the security deposit had already been taken out of my account, I'd already gotten the time off from my demanding tech job, and they'd so graciously paid for half the trip anyway. Most importantly, Lauryn's surprise proposal was going down at her birthday dinner on our last night, and she'd never let me live it down if I missed it. The only thing that had changed was not having Omar by my side to share the three-bedroom villa I'd rented. I just had to wrap my head around a different vacation than I initially thought I'd have. *Fuck,* I thought to myself. It was happening, and I was going.

Lauryn chimed in, jarring my thoughts. "Why pack a vibrator if you can have the real thing? Just curious."

I sucked my teeth. "Have we not just been on the phone for the past two hours talkin' about my sorry ass ex? Have you not been listening? I'm off men forever!"

Even though I couldn't see her, I could tell she was rolling her eyes. "Whatever, all I'm sayin' is there may be some fresh meat on the island. Shit, you know what they say, the best way to get over one man is to get under another!"

I lifted my shoulder in a half-shrug. "No thanks. I don't have the energy to fight for a nigga to love me anymore. I'm safer being lonely, it's fine."

"Then hang up the gloves, girl. And just have fun for once. You out here livin' like you in your fifties and you're not even thirty yet. You have the dream job, you have the means, and you a lil' baddie or whatever. So, what's the problem? You're worth the chase so let a mothafucka chase you for *once.*"

"If I'm even approached by a nigga on that island, I'm gonna tell him my relationship status is Netflix, Oreos, and these very comfortable sweatpants," I said, referring to the pants she'd already threatened to burn once.

She sighed with a slight chuckle. "I swear you're a lost cause."

"Don't worry, I'll make my flight to St. Martin."

"Now you swear on Big Mama's grave," she repeated back to me.

I huffed. "I swear."

two

. . .

Day One

CASSIDY

I whipped my car into the first available parking spot I could find inside the terminal garage. Normally, I would've parked in economy parking for long trips, but I was already rushing to get to airport in the first place. I hopped out of the car and popped the trunk while snatching off my scarf and rubbing the indented line off my forehead. You know, the one that screams *I just took my bonnet off, but my edges are now laid!*

My suitcase wheels rolled against the pavement as I shuffled through the airport, trying to get through checking my bags, security, and to my gate within thirty-two minutes. I nervously looked down at my watch every fifteen seconds as the minutes seemed to fly by. I couldn't wait to land in LAX to get on my connecting flight to St. Martin. The second I stepped onto the plane and took my seat in first-class, I let out a sigh of relief. I could finally fuckin' relax and officially start my vacation. While my girls were doing excursions with their men, I would be reading by the pool. While they were getting dicked down from sunup to sundown, I would be getting a Swedish massage from a male professional masseuse, and if I was lucky, he'd be something worth looking at. I meant what I said to Lauryn; I was going to make the best of my trip, come hell or high water.

During the plane change from LAX to St. Martin, I walked onto the smaller aircraft feeling better than better. The edible I'd eaten on my way to the airport had finally kicked in mid-flight, and I was feeling too good. I plopped down in my window seat and turned up the volume on my phone as Beyonce's *Party* blasted through my AirPods. Just as I started to bob my head and sway in my seat, I heard a familiar voice that instantly made my stomach churn.

"Yo, you in my seat."

I looked up just as the owner of that voice stationed himself in the aisle in front of me. There he was, both hell and high water in human form, Hendrix "The Tomb Raider" Croft. He tried his best to be inconspicuous with a black hoodie draped over his freshly cut fade, and sunglasses shielding his almond-shaped, cognac-brown eyes as to ward off the paparazzi or any screaming basketball fans hounding him for his autograph. He was a three-time NBA all-star and the bane of my existence since we were in high school.

My forehead puckered as I pulled my sunglasses away from my eyes. "What?"

"Seat 6A is mine. I got the window."

"Hendrix?"

"Oh shit, Cassidy? Cassidy Stokes? Is that you? You're the last person I expected to see here."

Time stopped, but he didn't. As much as it pained me to admit it, he looked better than words could describe. Just staring at the full licorice-colored beard covering his chin was enough to suck all the air out of my lungs down to the very last puff.

"It's a free country." I shrugged as I took a big gulp of the water bottle clutched in my hand.

"That's debatable. And you still in my seat though."

I rolled my irritated eyes. "Can you just let me sit here? I'm already buckled in."

"Nah, I need my window."

"Fine," I said, unhooking my seatbelt and switching over to the aisle seat. I pulled my knees in tight as he slid past me to sit by the window. As soon as he sat down, he closed the window shade. I quickly rolled my eyes. "Can you at least open it so I can see?"

"No."

My brows drew together. "Why not?"

"The fuck you need to see clouds for? This your first flight or somethin'?"

My eyes rolled toward the ceiling. "No, I just like to look. You got a problem with that?" I bit back.

"Nah, I don't. Maybe you'll catch 'em on your flight back," he said, sarcasm ringing deep in his voice.

I sat and stared at him in awe as he bared his straight, white teeth in my direction before

sliding his black and gold Beats by Dre headphones over the sparkling gold diamonds in his ear as a not too subtle attempt to tell me he was done talking. His smile was fuckin' lethal. I *hated* that I loved it. *Nope, don't look. Fuck these niggas, Cass. Fuck these niggas!* I chanted over and over inside my head. For the life of me, I couldn't understand why everyone kissed his ass, no matter how good it probably looked. *Hmph, it's probably just as bronzed and toned as the rest of his chiseled ass body,* I thought. As easy on the eyes as he was, I could tell he was going to be a menace to sit beside on a three-and-a-half-hour flight.

From the moment he was born, he was donned the Prince of Inglewood. Everyone who was anyone knew exactly who he was because his father, Jude Croft, was the king of the city and one of the biggest kingpins in Cali. So naturally, he was used to everything and everyone always orbiting around his ass. After his parents got divorced, him and his mom moved five houses down from me. Plus, he was Lauryn's brother's best friend. So even if I didn't run into him in my own neighborhood or in the hallways at school, I would most certainly have to see him whenever I went over Lauryn's house.

Like every other girl my age or older, I'd fallen under his spell and developed a stupid girlish crush on him. He used to give me goosebumps whenever I saw him until I heard him open his mouth for the first time. He'd made it painfully clear that he was nothing but a pompous asshole, and from the looks of it, shit hadn't changed. He was still used to the sun rising and sitting on his ass. His ass made the two years of high school went spent together my own personal hell, but it was a new day, and we were far from kids. He was going to be reminded that I wasn't the one.

Instead of entertaining his ass any longer, I turned my attention to the aisle and caught the eyes of the first flight attendant I could find. "Excuse me, are there any other seats available? They don't even have to be first-class at this point, I just need to switch seats. I'm willing to pay whatever."

"I'm sorry, ma'am, but this is a full flight. Can I get you a complimentary beverage or some ear plugs or something?"

"Um, yeah sure—just make it *strong*."

She bobbed her head up and down. "Got it."

Moments after we took off, he leaned his seat back. I sucked my teeth for the umpteenth time since he'd barged back into my life. The second I went to put my elbow on the armrest, I was blocked. "Do you have to take up both arm rests? There are other people on this plane besides you, you know?" I scoffed.

He sat up to pull off his hoodie. "You must've forgot you sittin' next to a full-size nigga," he said, with a hint of hood charisma laced in his voice.

His stretch allowed me to catch a glimpse of the tats on his biceps, triceps *goddamnceps*. At six-foot-four and a solid one-hundred and eighty pounds, he was built Ford tough. His sandy brown skin dripped with ink etched into his skin from his wrists all the way up to his neck. There were probably millions of women out there that would pay to be the camouflaged shirt resting against his skin, or the khaki cargo pants that didn't help to conceal the imprint of his dick laying lazily against his inner thigh.

As much as I despised him, I would never admit to him or anyone else that I'd followed bits and pieces of his career over the years. He was drafted his freshman year of college and had been in the league for about seven years. After bouncing around from team to team his first few years, he found his home with the Sin City Mambas as their starting point guard. He'd been with them for the past four years, hand delivering them two championship rings. He'd most recently gotten them to the finals and injured his knee in the sixth game, which put him out for the rest of the finals. Unlike his father, who was a household name in Inglewood, Hendrix was a household name in homes across the globe. As popular as he was, I always wondered why I never heard his name tied to any crazy scandals, baby mama drama, or serious relationships for that matter.

"Here you go, ma'am—your earplugs and your drink," the flight attendant said, snapping me out of my entranced thoughts about Hendrix. I never realized just how much I knew about someone I swore I couldn't stand.

"Can you actually bring me another one of these and a blanket as well?" I asked her.

She smiled, before tearing her eyes away from me to sneak a glance at the sleeping *Tomb Raider*. "Yeah...sure thing."

I shot her a quick smile before shaking my head. *Typical*, I figured. Before she could even make it back with my second drink and blanket, Hendrix had fallen into a slumber so deep, he'd started to snore.

"You've got to be fuckin' kidding me," I grumbled before jabbing my elbow into his arm. Three jabs later, he was still sleep and I was pissed. After downing two Irish Car Bombs back-to-back, all I could do was close my eyes, replace my AirPods with the earplugs the flight attendant had given me, and pray the liquor aided in drowning out his inconsiderate, snoring ass for the rest of the trip.

Midway through the flight, the turbulence from a passing thunderstorm had started to make me both nauseous and nervous. Nausea rolled through my stomach like a raging wave as the plane bounced and shook.

"Oh fuck," I whispered, slamming my eyes shut and clawing both armrests like a frightened feline.

With my eyes still closed, I began to say the Lord's Prayer inside my head. After that, I prayed that we wouldn't crash and that I didn't throw up all over myself or the arrogant nigga sucking up air beside me. My eyes jolted open the second I felt his warm hand on my thigh.

"Yo, chill. We gon' be straight," he assured.

Fever ran through my body as heat rose between my legs. I

couldn't form a thought, no less a sentence, and I knew my honey brown complexion had turned scarlet. I was torn between telling him to get his large hand off me or to keep it right where it was. One thing was for sure, if he kept his hand on my thigh for the rest of the way to the island, it was going to be the longest fuckin' flight ever.

"Fuck these niggas. Fuck these niggas. Fuck these niggas."

———

The second we landed, and I was able to get off the plane, I darted off like a lightning strike, trying to put as much distance between Hendrix and I as possible. He had no idea what he'd done to me, or maybe he did. Either way, I couldn't let that shit happen again. I was convinced that he was still an entitled jerk with even more money than he had when he was growing up. All I could do was pray that he was going to be tucked far away from me on the island.

After the driver from the resort put my luggage in the trunk, I sat in the cushioned leather backseat and instantly felt the cool air conditioning on full blast. After texting Lauryn to let her know I was on my way to the resort, I pulled my shades back over my eyes and let the hum of the engine and the smooth ride lull me to sleep.

The sound of the engine shutting off and the end of the blistering cold air blowing across my face, made me crack my eyes open. "Miss, we are here," the driver told me.

I shot him a quick smile before stretching. "Mmm, great. Thank you!"

"I will grab your bags and show you to the check-in area."

"That would be perfect, thanks!" I beamed, ready to really start my self-love vacay.

I followed him over to the desk with a pep in my step. "Hi, my name is Cassidy Stokes, and I'm checking in for a three-bedroom villa," I said as I approached the attendant behind the tall counter.

She flashed me a warm smile. "We are so happy to have you staying with us, Ms. Stokes. Please, tell me how long you'll be staying with us."

"Um, a week. I'm here with a bigger party, so my villa should be within the vicinity of theirs."

"Yes, our luxury villas come equipped with complimentary concierge service, a gardener, daily maid service, pool attendant, and property manager, should you have any questions or concerns during your stay. Check out is at noon, and I will go ahead and get you your villa information, just one second," she said, clicking away at her keyboard.

After watching her expression go from joy to confusion, I decided to speak up. "Um, is there something wrong?"

"Um, I'm not quite sure."

"What do you mean?"

"There seems to be some sort of mix-up."

"A mix-up?" I repeated.

"Yes, please just give me a second to figure this out."

"What seems to be the problem?" I quizzed.

"One second, ma'am," she reiterated before walking over to talk to another colleague.

I kissed my teeth as my posture immediately stiffened and heartrate quickened. *This cannot be fucking happening*, I thought to myself. My eyes were so busy staring daggers into the back of her head that I didn't even notice Hendrix take his place beside me at the counter.

"Well, well, well—we meet again."

I looked up just as he paraded that stupid fuckin' breathtaking smile in my direction. His overwhelming body stature didn't help either. My five-foot-four physique was completely swallowed up in his shadow. He was like a tree I suddenly wanted to climb. This nigga was just *too fine* for his own good. His presence had taken the wind out of my sails for sure. Instead of returning the friendly gesture or offering up a reply, I turned my attention back to the attendant who'd seemingly left me hanging.

"Sir, I can take you over here," another attendant called out to him.

He sucked his teeth and shot me a final glance. "Guess I'll see your rude ass around."

three

. . .

HENDRIX

Cassidy Stokes was a *raging bitch.*

There, I said it.

She was the last person I expected to run into, and by the way she'd been rolling her neck at me since the plane ride, I could tell she felt the same. First, she zoomed off the plane in a huff, then the second I pulled up to the resort, I saw her ass fussing. I didn't know who the hell put that big ass chip on her shoulder, but that shit was off-putting as hell. I wasn't going to feed into her bullshit when I had my own shit to deal with. Not only was I recovering from a knee injury that took me out for the rest of the finals, but I'd also been dealing with the embarrassment and shame of being traded to one of the worst teams in the whole fuckin' league.

I'd always had dreams of shooting hoops. People started callin' me The Tomb Raider my freshman year in high school. I was the only freshman on the varsity team, and it didn't take long for niggas to realize I was the reason the stands were packed every Friday night. I got busy on that fuckin' court, and everybody knew it. How I'd gone from an NBA all-star making over 40,000,000 dollars a year to being thrown away like I was a piece of trash had my head all the way fucked-up. To me, it was the equivalent to getting picked last for kick-ball teams on the playground. I came to St. Martin to lick my wounds in peace and put the focus back on my career, not go blow-for-blow with a chick from high school.

Growing up, her cousin, Mark, was my best friend, so I would see her whenever I went over to his house. I'd always thought she was bad, and out of all the girls that were on my dick back then, I could honestly say Cassidy wasn't one of them. From the moment I met Cassidy, she'd always had a wall up. Even after me and my mom moved into her neighborhood, she never gave me anything but attitude, so I masked my feelings for her and was an asshole in return. As a kid in the spotlight, I didn't have the time nor the know how to break it down. And from the looks of it, the shit had only gotten tougher over the years.

As soon as I handed the attendant my I.D., the attendant that had been helping Cassidy walked over. "I'm sorry, sir. But um, there's been a mix-up in the system."

"What kind of mix-up?" I asked for clarity as I looked down at my phone.

I'd been trying to get in contact with my agent for the last two days, yet it seemed like every time my phone vibrated, there was a different sports headline with my name in it. Whether it was TMZ, ESPN, or some other annoyin' ass paparazzi with a camera in my face or gossip blog with my name in their mouths, I could feel the heat on me. Throughout life, I'd been used to being able to write my own ticket, whether it was because of who my father was or how good I was at ball. Without ball, I would be nothing.

"Well, it seems your villa has been double booked with another guest. Her, actually," she said, pointing to Cassidy.

"*Cassidy?*" I asked, my neck shooting up as my forehead wrinkled in disbelief.

Her brows snapped together as soon as she heard me call her name. "I'm sorry, what?"

"Can't you just put her somewhere else?" I asked.

She put her hands on her hips. "No, they can move you! I was here first!"

"Move me?"

"Yes, move you! You can go anywhere, Hendrix. Why do you have to stay here? All I am trying to do is have a nice fucking relaxing ass vacation *alone*, that's it!"

"I'm trying to do the same shit, so why don't we just split it? Your little ass don't need all that space anyway."

She smacked her juicy, watermelon pink lips. "And you do? Just because I'm not a fuckin' celebrity like you don't mean I don't make my own money. I'm allowed to ball out and enjoy the fruits of my labor just like you are. You're not the only one with bread, here."

"Um, ma'am, if you agree to that, we will refund you both fifty-percent of what you paid for your stay," one of the attendants chimed in.

Cassidy huffed before pulling her eyes up to mine. "Fine, but just because we're practically being forced to share the same space for the next few days doesn't mean I have to like it, when I could just easily pretend like you don't exist."

"Okay, we'll um, go ahead and process the refunds for both of you and call your car around to have your driver take you to your villa. We are so sorry for the mix-up, and we hope you enjoy your stay."

"Um, no. I want my own car. I'm not sharing with him," she demanded.

I scoffed. If she couldn't stand sitting next to me for a ten-minute ride, I didn't know how we were going to make it through the week.

"Separate cars is not a problem, ma'am. I will make the arrange-ments now," she replied with a smile.

I bobbed my head. "Thanks," I told them.

"Yeah, thanks," Cassidy said before stalking off.

———

"What is it that you do, anyway?" I asked as I stepped up beside her, waiting for our drivers to pull around.

She shot me a cold stare with her arms folded across her chest. "Are you serious right now? Don't talk to me."

"Yeah, I'm serious. I mean, your ass made such a big deal back there about how you can ball out if you feel like it, I figured I'd ask."

She narrowed her eyes at me and flared her nostrils. "If you must know, I'm in computer security. Something that takes a little bit more brainpower than dribbling a ball."

I chuckled. "Oh, word? That's how you goin'?"

She gave a lazy shrug. "I said what I said."

"I guess that computer shit is cool or whatever."

"Well, not all of us have the height and a solid jump shot like you. I had to scrape to get enough money to put me through school while people like you got the red carpet rolled out for them."

I rolled my eyes before stepping up and towering over her petite ass frame. She needed to be put in her place, and since she kept slanging her attitude my way and letting slick shit fall off her tongue, I was going to be the one to do it. "Yo, I've been tryna be cool with your self-pitying ass, but you gon' watch your fuckin' mouth when you address me, Cassidy. I may be a mothafuckin' ball player, but you know where the fuck I come from, and that street shit is gon' always be in me, aight? We already agreed we gon' split this shit up, so you stay your lil' ass on your side, and I'll stay on mine." I gritted my teeth.

"You should be grateful I'm even agreeing to this shit in the first place!" she snapped, just like an Inglewood girl. On the low, I was still a sucker for that hood shit.

I scoffed. "You want my gratitude? Nah, you ain't earned that yet," I declared before leaving her ass standing there with her pretty ass mouth hanging wide open.

The moment I was on my way to the villa, I began to chuckle at the irony of the whole situation. I'd left the fuckin' country to clear my head and destress, yet I was going to have to share my space with the most stressful woman I'd ever met in my life. From the moment I saw her on that plane, I knew it was going to be some shit between us and arguing back wouldn't do anything but fan the flame. We'd already started the day off with tension thick enough to slice with a knife, and I knew that spending the next six days with her could easily turn into the week from hell.

A part of me smiled at the idea of getting to play her close for a week. As rowdy as she was, there wasn't a flaw to her French-tipped toes. Her long braids competed in length with her smooth legs that had been kissed by sun to be the perfect shade of honey brown. She had perky breasts that were real and a nice bubble booty. Any woman that got with me had to have a set of childbearing hips because my seed was gon' be no less than ten pounds, and she had 'em. If it wasn't for her poor ass attitude, staying away from her would be hard, but I planned to keep my distance until I couldn't anymore.

four

. . .

CASSIDY

Our cars approached the gated entrance and pulled up to the villa within seconds of each other. Hendrix took one look at me when he stepped out, and I was set on fire—not in a good way. I'd never been around someone whose presence intrigued and repelled me all at once. My equilibrium was thrown off when I was around him, and I figured the faster I got inside, the faster I could get away from him. I tried to keep my focus on the beautiful palm trees, clear, blue skies, lush gardening, and shimmering blue pool ahead of me as I sped up my pace. Without bothering to say excuse me, I bumped past him and lost my balance.

"Oh shit!" I squeaked before stumbling and crashing into the pool.

I made the biggest, loudest, *most utterly embarrassing* splash as my entire body submerged underwater. Seconds later, I popped back up only to see Hendrix's arm outstretched to me at the edge of the pool.

"Oh shit, I'm glad your rude ass can swim. I thought I was gonna have to jump in there and save you," he said, before flashing me his stupid ass, breathtaking smirk.

I wanted to smack that shit right off his face, but instead, I slapped his hand away and pulled myself out of the water. I was sopping wet from head to toe, looking about as attractive as a dog caught in the middle of a tsunami. I bent down to swipe up my phone that I'd dropped before hitting the water.

"You could've ruined my phone!" I yelled, swatting wet braids out of my face, "and what if I couldn't swim, huh?"

"But you clearly can, and this pool don't go deeper than six feet anyway. I think you would've been aight."

I huffed and narrowed my eyes. "Whatever, just stay your ass away from me, or I swear to God!" I said, balling up my fists.

He must've felt the heat radiating off my body because he took a few steps back and let me enter the villa first. I stormed down the hall in a blitz of anger, zooming past the long, U-shaped beige couch and large, floor-to-ceiling windows in the living room that overlooked the Caribbean Sea and let the sun in from all angles. All I wanted to do was find the master suite and settle my fucking nerves. A subtle smile crept across my face when I stepped into the room and saw those same floor-to-ceiling windows with a view of the turquoise waves rolling up against the smooth shore. Hearing the waves crashing against one another was like music to my ears. All I wanted to do was marry my body to the plush California king bed, but I kept trekking my wet ass across the marble floors into the bathroom.

Hundreds of droplets of warm water sprang out of the large rainfall showerhead. After I made sure I'd gotten clean, I popped the bottle of champagne I'd found inside the welcome basket on top of my bed and drew myself a warm bath to soak and further settle my nerves.

"Cheers to a week of self-love," I mumbled to myself before clanking the champagne flute against the bottle and submerging my body beneath the warm suds.

It was just my damn luck to spend the entire week trapped with someone on my shit list. As a matter of fact, he was at the tip top. There was no way I was taking my ass back to San Jose or staying at another resort, so I only had one choice—share a villa with the nigga and minimize my interactions with his fine ass as much as possible.

───────

I'd soaked long enough for both my fingers and toes to prune and the water to go lukewarm, and yet I still wasn't ready to get out. Instead, I reached over to edge of the tub to swipe up my phone and call Lauryn.

"Um, I thought I told you to call me when you got to the resort!" she barked as soon as she picked up the phone.

"Girl! I would have, but shit has been crazy all day long! It's literally been the day from hell!"

"Ah hell, what happened?"

I sighed. "I don't know if you'll believe me when I tell you."

"Try me."

"Well first of all, I almost missed my damn flight rushing to the airport. Then, I make it to LAX, I get on my connecting flight in first class and guess who, of all people, the Lord himself picked to sit beside me?"

"Oh shit, who, Cass?"

"Fucking Hendrix!"

"Wait, Hendrix? Like, Hendrix, Hendrix?"

"Yes, that nigga, Hendrix!"

Lauryn burst out into a roar of laughter. "Ooooh shiiiiiiiitttttttt, Cass! Boy, would I love to have been a fly on the wall watching you two interact after all these years."

"That's not even the worst part! Not only do I have to sit next to this nigga the whole way here, but when I get here and try to check in, guess who I see?"

"Get the fuck out of here."

"Hold your comments until the end, bitch. It gets worse!"

"What? He stayin' in the villa next to yours or something?"

"Try the same villa."

"Hold up, what? What do you mean the same villa?"

"I got here and I go to check in, and then they tell me there's been a mix-up in the system, and they have both of us double booked for the same fuckin' villa. Of course he couldn't be a fuckin' gentleman and just take something else! So since neither wanted to give up the villa, boom, here we are."

Lauryn gasped. "Stop lying!"

"See! I told you that your ass wouldn't fuckin' believe me."

"Are you for real?"

I shook my head. "As real as a fuckin' heart attack, bitch."

"So, you're telling me that he's in the same villa with you…right… now?"

"I guess that nigga around here somewhere. I scared his ass off after that pool incident. Fuckin' with me, he better watch his ass over the next few days." I scoffed.

"Hold up, what pool incident?"

"He tried to drown me!"

"He what?"

I huffed. "Okay, not literally, but he knocked me in the pool. Well, I bumped into him and kinda fell, really. I was drenched from head to toe. My phone almost got ruined!"

I knew I technically couldn't blame him for me falling in the pool, but I could blame him for being in my space.

"So, did he push you or did your clumsy ass fall?" she asked for clarity.

"I fell, but it's not like he tried to save me or anything!"

"Would you have wanted him to?" she quizzed.

"Hell no!" I barked.

It was safer to hate him, to hate all men. Anything with a dick and balls, really. I didn't discriminate.

"Exactly, so what you complaining for?"

"Because I don't want to share my space with that nigga for the rest of the week!" I whined.

"I get it, girl, but don't be too hard on him."

"Why not? He was always a dick to me, and you know it!"

Lauryn let out a soft chuckle. "Your ass wasn't nothin' nice either, bitch. Don't front."

I rolled my eyes. "Whatever."

"But nah, Cass, I'm serious. Go easy on him. He's been through a lot lately."

"Girl, bye. Like what? What could be so wrong in his perfect little world?"

"Well, for one—you know he's coming off that injury that took him out of the finals, and two, I know you heard about that nigga gettin' traded."

My lips downturned. "I knew about his knee, but I didn't hear the bit about the trade. But, I mean—it's not like he got fired, right? He's a ball player. Those niggas get traded like Pokémon cards all time."

She snickered. "Yeah, but the way he found out about the trade was embarrassing as hell. TMZ caught him coming out of physical therapy and started bombarding him with questions about how he felt about being traded to one of the worst teams in the league before the Mambas even got a chance to call and tell him personally."

"Oh shit," I mumbled, sinking further into the cool bath water.

"Yeah, Mark said they talked not too long after it happened and he was pretty fucked-up about it."

"Damn, really?"

"Um, ball is that nigga's life, Cass. You know that."

I kissed my teeth and mumbled, "Fuck."

Lauryn's words made me quickly realize what I'd said to him earlier was condescending. The emotional salvage yard that was once my heart had me talking savage as fuck and acting completely out of my character. I never had a problem putting him in his place, but I would've never kicked him if I'd known he was already down.

"What?" Lauryn asked.

"Ugh," I groaned, "I might've said something about how it didn't require a lot of brainpower to play basketball to him during an argument when we were checking in."

"Cass!"

"I know! I'm sorry, I didn't know, and I was just so damn mad at the time, I just said whatever was on my mind."

"You need to go and apologize to that man!"

"I'd honestly rather just come to your villa and chill for a bit," I said, trying to change subjects.

"Girl, listen, we are still *so tired*. We got off the plane and got here and took showers and a nap, and we are still in this comfortable ass bed."

"Damn, I knew it! I knew that shit was comfortable the moment I saw it!"

"Yeah, girl. It's got a hold on both of us, I'm sorry. But maybe dinner tomorrow?"

"Fine. This week is about my healing anyway, so I'll get a jumpstart on it by finding out what this California king talkin' bout."

"Yasss! You better go enjoy those snuggles, girl! I'll see you soon. Love you."

"Yeah, yeah. Bye," I mumbled before ending the call.

Once I climbed out of the tub and dried off, I crawled in the bed and found the video TMZ posted of when they bombarded Hendrix the day of his trade announcement. Lauryn was right; just from watching the video I was embarrassed for him. I couldn't imagine how he felt being the subject of endless gossip and opinion about his future of his career. It became clear to me that we were both in a dark place and if we were both going to make it out alive at the end of the week, then I was going to have to keep my words and my hands to myself. I didn't like confrontation for real, but the shit coming my way had me unraveled and ready to swing at life like Cuba Gooding Jr's ass in *Boyz in the Hood*. I toyed with the idea of apologizing or just letting bygones be just that. In the end, I decided to sleep on it and if we were both still breathing the next morning, *then* I'd apologize, *maybe*.

five

. . .

Day Two

CASSIDY

The sun's warmth was set to a perfect seventy-five degrees, and there was a cool breeze coming off the water as I made my way back up the private walking path from the beach to the villa. It was a new day and while all my friends were out on couples excursions, I started on my path to self-healing by watching the sunrise and doing morning yoga on the beach. I felt relaxed as the Zen energy radiated off my body. I decided to keep the vibe going and grab a bite to eat while I relaxed on one of the oversized couches out on the pool terrace and listened to the waves gently crash against the soft, white sand of Plum Bay Beach.

I walked through the sliding glass door leading back inside and tip-toed across the white marble floor in the full gourmet kitchen, looking for the menu to see what the chef services offered. There were pans hanging from the ceiling overtop an oversized island and stainless-steel appliances. Adjacent to the breakfast bar was an eight-seater dining room table with the menu binder on it. The entire room was filled with beautiful wooden artifacts and trendy décor laced with island colors. It was almost as if you could feel the warm, tropical breeze from just simply standing in a room. With such inviting views, I didn't know which part of the beautiful space had the better vantage point. Everything was gorgeous.

After looking over the menu, I decided to eat light instead and poured myself a glass of freshly squeezed orange juice and plucked a few pieces of fruit in a bowl from the exotic fruit platter sitting on the kitchen counter. While sitting outside, I pulled my sunglasses over my eyes and tossed my head back before flinging a piece of fruit between my lips.

"Self-love is the best love," I chanted as I pulled out my phone and looked on the resort's app for which in-villa spa services I was going to treat myself to. My fingertips swiped through the pages as I went back and forth, trying to decide whether I wanted the holistic Swedish massage or holistic aromatherapy massage.

"Yo, have you seen the menu? I'm starving," a sweaty, shirtless Hendrix asked.

From the beads of sweat racing down his temple to the eight flexed, latte brown abs invading my peace and my quiet, it was clear to see he'd just finished working out. I paused, selfishly taking him all in with my shaded eyes before uttering my first syllable. Simply put, he was too delicious not to look at.

"Good morning to you too."

"I didn't know we were being cordial. Last time I saw you, your wet ass had your fist balled up at me."

I sighed, knowing it was practically now or never. "About yester-day...I'm—"

"Yeah, about yesterday. Your rude ass needs to apologize."

I rolled my eyes. As usual, he was two steps behind me. I didn't need him to tell me what to do. "Hmm...damn, it's right on the tip of my tongue, and I can't think of it. I hate when that happens," I said, while tapping the side of my head.

"Let me help you out. It starts with the letter 'S'."

"I'm s—I'm ssss—orry? There, I said it."

Hendrix drew in a frustrated breath. "You better stop fuckin' with me, Cassidy."

"Or else what?"

His lips twisted as he turned to walk back inside. I quickly jumped up to follow him. "Hey, okay, okay. wait. I'm sorry, okay? I shouldn't have said what I said about my career being harder than yours. I'm positive I couldn't get out there and dribble a ball with precision the way you do. It was condescending and I—I'm sorry for that."

"That's all you're sorry for?" he quizzed.

I defensively folded my arms across my chest. "Excuse me? Is there something else I should be sorry for?"

He squared off his shoulders. "How about being a bitch to me since the moment I stepped on the plane and sat next to your ass?"

"*Bitch?* Who the fuck you callin' a bitch?" I yelled, sending any ounce of Zen I had left flying right out.

"There you go with that shit. I never said that."

I scoffed. "Close enough."

"Your ass stay on the defense."

"So?"

"So, chill. All I wanted was the fuckin' menu. If you don't know where that's at then that's all your miserable ass had to say," he barked before leaving me standing in the middle of the floor.

six

. . .

HENDRIX

I'd had just about all I could take of Cassidy, and we'd only been sharing a space for less than forty-eight hours. I was already on ten about my agent ghosting me and dodging my calls like the plague, and I didn't need her shit added to it. As pretty as it was, Cassidy's mouth was the type to make a nigga turn to Jesus or want to send her head flying off her freckled shoulders.

I found the menu without her help and took it into the living room with me and turned on the TV. Of course, one of the first things I saw when I put it on ESPN was my name across the screen as the two on-air commentators discussed my injury, my trade, and the fate of my career.

"Count him out if you want to, but he's not called The Tomb Raider for nothing. Hendrix Croft gets busy on the court, okay? Anyone can see that he loves the game. He's true to it and although his season didn't end on a high note, he had an amazing start to his season. I think he'll be back on top."

"I'll have to agree to disagree with you, Samantha. It's sad to say, but the guy just may be old news. Let's be honest, here. He's a great player, but he's

no Lebron. He's been traded to one of the historically worst teams in the league. We all know that's where players go when their careers are on life support. This just isn't a good look for him, especially with all the new hot talent that some of these new players have."

"Let me tell you one thing, Kansas City broke the bank to get The Tomb Raider, so I'm not going to be surprised if he gets in there and does just what he did with the Sin City Mambas. He'll be looking at another championship ring soon, John, just wait."

I quickly changed the channel when I heard the slight tap of footsteps across the floor and mentally braced myself for the drama that I was sure would soon ensue.

"I see you found the menu," she stated.

"Yup," I said, without bothering to turn and face her.

"Hey, um...I just wanted to apologize again about the whole dribbling a ball thing I said. I—I didn't know about the trade."

I huffed. "Everybody in the whole word knows about the shit by now, I'm just tryna deal with it."

"And how's that going?" she inquired.

I scoffed as I finally turned my head to look at her. "Like you care."

"For the millionth time, I'm sorry. I didn't know your situation before I said anything."

I nodded. "Sometimes, I sit back and think about how different my life was a year ago, shit, even three months ago. I was at the top of my game. I had respect, or at least I thought I did. I bled black and red for the past four years. I made that team a whole fuckin' franchise and they traded me? Me!"

"And you didn't see this coming at all? Like, there were no warning signs?"

"Don't you know it's all about the all-mighty dollar to these greedy mothafuckas? They own sports teams because they want to work us until one of these million-dollar body parts fail. The moment it does, they start working to replace you, because you're a liability and no longer an asset."

"You don't know if that's the reason," she rebutted.

"Shit, everything was all good. Mothafuckas were smiling in my face, talking about renegotiating contracts with my agent, new endorsement deals, and boom, I get a grade two partial tear of my MCL in my left knee in game six of the finals, and two months later, I get hit with the news I'm being traded like I'm a piece of trash. They don't need any other reason than that to try and kill my career. I know they blamed that loss on me."

Her lips flattened into a hard line. "Who? How? You put half the points on the board that night."

"Nobody said it to my face, but what other explanation could there be? I put that team on my back and built them up to where they are now, and they did me like that? I'm pushing thirty, Cassidy. I should be writing my own ticket by now, and yet I'm being passed around like a slut at a frat party, and to be honest, I don't want new teammates or to make new friends."

It was no secret that I'd had a rough time finding a home when I first entered the league. Either my attitude didn't mesh with the other teammates, or they just didn't have the work ethic to match mine. I'd gone from team to team until finding my groove in Las Vegas, and I was scared to have to start all over again.

She folded her arms across her chest. "You know what you sound like right now?"

"What?"

"A fuckin' middle schooler or something, Hendrix."

I shook my head. "I wouldn't expect you to understand. Every time I turn on the fuckin' TV or look at my phone, niggas got me out here lookin' like a joke."

"So, make sure you're the one who has the last laugh," she declared.

"How, when I have to play on a team that hasn't been to a single championship since 1987, and their best player averages maybe eight points a game?"

"Well, maybe it's time for you to go there with your head held high and show everybody who doubted you just what you can do. You already said you made the Mambas a franchise in four years, right?

What makes you think you can't do that in Kansas City with your new team in less time than that?"

I responded with a shrug even though I knew she was right. Rising to leadership meant there was a bullseye on my back, and I wasn't going to let that shit stop me from making my own rules no matter whose jersey I wore in the upcoming season. Even on vacation, I made sure I still got in as much of a vigorous workout as I could without my physical therapist around, and when it was time to pack up and head out to Kansas, I'd be in perfect condition and ready to play my heart out.

"Am I right or am I right?" Cassidy asked, waiting for a verbal response.

"You are."

"To quote my favorite movie, 'Life's funny sometimes. You just don't want it laughin' at you,'" she claimed.

"Your favorite movie *The Wood*? I probed.

She shrugged her lean shoulders. "You can't be from Inglewood and not have that at least in your top five favorite movies of all time," she declared.

I bobbed my head in agreeance. "Shit, you right. That's my favorite movie, too. What's your favorite line?"

"That's a hard question and you know it. That shit had way too many iconic lines."

"First one that comes to mind, then," I tested her.

"Aight, aight. Um," she paused, "'you think my sister a hoe or somethin'? You think she a fuckin' toy!'" she yelled.

I threw my hands up in defense. "Nah, man I think she purdy!" I replied, pretending to be the young, country-ass Mike from the flashback with him and Stacey in the movie.

My neck tossed back with laughter, ridding the air of all the awkward tension we'd built up with a simple shared interest.

After we'd come down from our shared laugh, she spoke up again. "You wanna know what I remember?"

"What?"

"The game right before the winter formal, like my sophomore year or something. You guys were down like thirty points and you'd sprained your—"

"Right wrist in the second quarter," I added.

"Yup, and what did you do?"

"Shit, I kept playing. I couldn't let us go out like that."

"I remember actually feeling bad for you because I could see how much pain you were in just by looking at you, but you wouldn't give up. You just kept playing your little heart out."

"Don't get it twisted, ain't nothin' about me little, but I feel you. We went on to dog they asses by like twenty points in the end, too," I boasted.

"Exactly. So, if you didn't give up with a sprained wrist, why are you giving up so easily now?" she probed.

Cassidy laid it on thick, but it was the shit I needed to hear. I could tell myself the same shit a million times a day, but it hit different coming from someone else's mouth. Most of the people around me were more concerned about how the trade would affect my money instead of me. Who knew Cassidy would have been the first and only one to make me feel good about the next change in my career.

"Nah, you right. You're absolutely right. Fuck that shit, I'll be back on top soon!"

"I'm sure you will. How's your knee by the way?"

Her question made me look down at it and rub it gently. "It's good, getting better every day. No pain. Doc and my physical therapist cleared me to come out on this trip. I've just been laying up for the past four weeks resting and shit. Hot water really makes it feel good after a workout, and I've got the perfect view of the water from my shower."

"Oh, yeah?"

"Yeah, since your ass took the master suite, I guess they figured they'd put the better bathroom in another room. But it's all glass and open for the world to see."

"The beach outside our villa is private."

"Good, because I don't need the next TMZ headline to be about pictures of my dick." I chuckled.

She smirked. "Yeah, we wouldn't want that."

"Aight, well I'm about to go hit up that shower now. Thanks for the pep talk, Cass."

seven

. . .

Day Three

CASSIDY

I'd woken up to see the sun sitting over the Caribbean Sea for the second day in a row and was still completely in awe. If I could bottle it up and take it back home to Cali, then I would. Instead, I rolled over and grabbed my phone to take a picture from the balcony outside my bedroom.

"This is so beautiful," I mumbled as my eyes oscillated around the beauty in front of me. The glistening, turquoise waters ran for miles. My neck sluggishly lurched to the right, and my entire body froze up like a glacier. There, in all his glory, Hendrix stood in his boxed-out glass shower that overlooked the ocean just like he said it did. He was also right when he said he had the better bathroom. My eyes continued down his body, devouring the length of him. His tatted torso was almost completely covered in ink. I studied the curve of his biceps as he pressed his hand against the glass fogging up by the second. Seconds later, I saw his abs flex as his right hand curved around his long, hard dick.

"Oh shit," I muttered, eyes glued to the vision.

My bottom lip practically grazed against my chin, hanging open wide. Any doubt I had prior about what Hendrix Croft had swinging in between his legs had been put to rest. What he possessed was enough to break up families. His teeth gripped his bottom lip as he continued to stroke the caramel monster I was sure he should've had both hands on. My thighs quivered, but as embarrassed as I was, I couldn't tear my eyes away for one second. I felt like a complete animal for watching, *gawking even*, as my pussy thumped like the drums in a HBCU marching band. The longer I watched, the juicier the inside of my thighs became. I observed his sexy, seat of a face, suddenly aching in lust a dozen feet away. As turned on as I was, I couldn't help but feel a twinge of curiosity. I wanted to know what it was like to get fucked with *that*; *dogged* by that. As internally frustrated as I was, I secretly welcomed the release. *I can't be back up on my bullshit so soon after a breakup, can I?* I thought to myself.

My heart stopped the moment his eyes focused on mine. I could only imagine the thoughts racing through his head. I quickly tore my eyes away and swiped my disheveled hair out of my face before dodging back inside. I couldn't stand to be in the path of his vision any longer. I was completely mortified, yet extremely horny. My feet quickened over to my suitcase as I flipped it upside down over my bed and spilled the contents out in search of my vibrator. Once I locked eyes on the purple lifesaver, I darted into the bathroom and locked the door behind me. My heartrate throbbed just as violently as my pussy. *Maybe there was a slight chance he didn't see me*, I thought as I turned on the shower and stripped down. A cold shower and a quick masturbation session were my safest bets to cool the fire that the sight of him ignited in me.

Thoughts nastier than porn raced through my head as I imagined every inch of him inside me. After I came three times back-to-back, I let the shower water heat up and cleansed my body from head to toe. I had defeated the beast, if only momentarily. I had to put the focus back on keeping my composure around him because the more time I spent around him, I unraveled like a cheap spool of yarn. Twenty minutes later, I stepped out of the foggy bathroom only to have Hendrix's voice hit my ears before my eyes were greeted by his presence. He was live and in color and sitting on the edge of my bed.

"Did you enjoy the show?" he queried.

eight

. . .

HENDRIX

She stopped dead in her tracks when she saw me perched on the edge of her bed amongst all the other things flung across it.

"I don't know what you're talking about," she said, tightening her grasp on the plush, white bathrobe clinging to her naked body.

I smirked. It was clear she was both flustered and embarrassed. "I saw you watching me."

"Please, don't flatter yourself. Nobody was lookin' at you. I barely saw anything."

"Yeah, aight. Whatever you say, but we both know you're curious."

She chuckled. "Boy, bye! Why would I be curious? It's not my first time seeing a dick."

"I thought you said you barely saw anything," I reminded her.

She sucked her teeth. "Whatever. Can you get out of my room so I can get dressed?"

"Oh, so you kicking me out when you were the one invading my privacy in the first place?"

Cassidy scoffed. "What? You think I'll run straight to TMZ with whatever I saw or somethin'? Boy, please. I'm not one of these lil' groupies or somebody out here lookin' for a quick come-up," she said, flinging her long braids to the back.

I smirked. I enjoyed pressing her buttons. "I never said you were."

"Besides, if anybody should be mad, it's me. Or do I need to remind you about the little pool incident a couple days ago? I was soaking wet!"

"Mmm," I mumbled.

"What?" she asked, folding her arms across her chest.

"Nothin'."

"Say it!" she demanded.

I rose from the side of her bed and headed for the door. "That's the second time this week you've blamed me for getting you *wet*," I said, before showing myself out.

Her wall of emotional protection wasn't the only thing I was trying to beat down, but I would save it for when she was ready.

———

I woke up from a nap to my phone vibrating. I'd been calling my sorry ass agent for days. and he'd finally decided to return my calls.

"Max, how convenient of you to return my calls when I'm out of the country," I answered with sarcasm coursing through my tone.

"It's not like that, Hendrix. It's just—"

"It's just what? Business? Is that why you were urging me to get out of town two weeks ago? Did you know this trade shit was coming?" I scolded him.

"No, not at all. I was just as blindsided as you were about the news."

I scoffed. "Bullshit."

"C'mon, you know me, Hendrix."

"I thought I did, but when it came time for you to do your fuckin' job, you put me on the backburner like one of your D-list fuckin' clients when you know I've made you the most money!"

"I understand your frustration, and I—"

"I pay you to put out fires and when shit was burning down all around me, where the fuck was your white ass at, huh!" I yelled into the receiver. "I swear to God if I find out you knew and you didn't tell me, I'm going to smack the dog shit out of you when I see you again!" I warned him.

"Look, I know you're feeling extremely undervalued right now and probably saying things you don't mean, but I still appreciate you as a client, and I'm still here fighting with and for you, Hendrix. What benefits you, benefits me, remember?"

"Then you need to start acting like it instead of having me leave you ten voicemails, trying to figure out where the hell you were."

"I know, and I apologize for that. I should've had my office reach out to you and tell you that I'd gone out of the country with my family, and I turned my phone off."

My eyes rolled to the back of my head. All I heard coming out of his mouth was excuse after excuse. "Yeah, whatever."

He sighed. "Listen, my advice to you is to enjoy your vacation. Take this down time to relax and get your head back in the game."

"My head has always been in the game, and I don't need you to give me advice, Max. I need you to do what I pay you to do and tell me you have some good news for me. A new endorsement deal, a new negotiation, something."

"Just hear me out, Hendrix, because I've been underground trying to work some new shit out for you, okay?"

"And?"

"And, I have good news and bad news." He sighed.

"I can't take no more bad news, Max," I admitted.

"The bad news is, your endorsement deal with Nike just ended and they have decided not to renew…"

"Fuck!" I yelled, about ready to fling the phone into the depths of the Caribbean Sea.

"Listen! The good news is, right now, I'm in talks with Adidas and Gatorade, and there's been some chatter with Subway as well. I'm working on the next big thing for you, which is a lifetime endorsement deal. The five years you spent with Nike were great, but I know you want bigger. And we both know a lifetime deal is an athlete's wet dream!" he boasted.

"Okay, so what happens now? What are they saying?" I asked.

"Well, nothing is in the bag just yet, but trust me, as soon as you get back in town, it's back to appearances, interviews, and meetings. My goal is to have some new contracts coming your way in the next couple of weeks!"

I could hear his salesy tongue slithering through the other end of the phone. All I could do was shake my head. Until something was final, I didn't trust shit he had to say.

"But endorsements aside, now that the news is out about your trade, you should be expecting a call from the Kansas City coach in the next week or so. Whether you believe it or not, we all want to make sure you're the most comfortable in your new position there."

"Yeah, aight."

"I'm serious, Hendrix. We all want the best for you," he assured me.

"I just don't have time for a waste of time, Max. So, when you start showing me some shit that benefits me and I ain't talkin' about this hypothetical, maybe someday bullshit. I'm talkin' concrete, sign my name on the dotted line shit, then we can talk. Until then, let the coach know I'll be awaiting his call," I said before pressing the red button and ending the call.

Growing up with street money meant I'd always been hard to impress. For much of my life, money was no object. After my parents got divorced, and I became the man of the house, I had to make sure I kept myself focused on my game so I could make it big and keep my mom used to the lifestyle she'd been living for years as the Queen of Inglewood. By the time I was going into my senior year in high school, I had already accepted a full ride to the University of Southern California to play basketball. After spending my freshman year there, I entered the draft. At five o'clock that evening, I got selected as a first round draft pick. By nine o'clock that same evening, my father's house was being raided, and he was being hauled off to prison. Suddenly, my entire family started looking at me like the new cash cow since the drug money stopped coming in.

Early on, I learned that the people I called my friends and family only cared about what I could give them. Over the years, only a select few gave enough fucks to call and check on me at random or wish me a happy birthday. If I wasn't writing a check or dropping off a care package whenever I dropped into town, they didn't want to hear from me. The only person who had ever looked out for me and never asked for a single dime was spending the rest of his life behind bars.

nine

. . .

Day Four

CASSIDY

Grips on your waist, front way, back way, you know that I don't play, Drake's voice crooned through the Bluetooth speaker as the private yacht my girls and I chartered set sail across the glistening, pristine water. Aside from the captain, there wasn't a dick in sight, and I couldn't have been happier. Lauryn, my girls, Brielle and Shauna, and I were in for a half-day of snorkeling, jet skis, and straight good vibes. Our squad was draped in all white bikinis, giving off serious Black girl magic vibes will all different shades of brown between us.

"Look what I've got, ladies," Brielle cheered, waving a Ziploc bag in the air.

Lauryn's freshly waxed brows shot up. "What the fuck is that?"

"It's a weed brownie, bitch!"

"Brielle, you brought drugs here!" I blurted out.

"Shh! You goddamn opp! All loud and shit! Here, everybody break off a piece, eat it, and wash it down with a shot of tequila. Are we on vacation or not? Let's start acting like it, bitchesssss!" she squealed, before turning around to do a quick twerk to Drake's *One Dance* blaring through the Bluetooth speaker.

Shauna shrugged while swiping her burgundy-tipped dreadlocks out of her face. "I'm in."

Lauryn looked at me and then back at Brielle, who held the brownie in hand. "Fine, fuck it."

"You in, Cass?" Brielle asked, coaxing me.

"Fuck it." I shrugged. "Who would've thought a quarter of a weed brownie and shots of Case Migos would be my breakfast?"

"It's the breakfast of fuckin' champions, bitch!" Brielle hailed, smacking her fruit-scented lips together.

Forty minutes later, we were all high as shit out in the middle of the sea, getting white girl wasted and having the time of our lives. With a mimosa glued to my right hand, I laid out on the front of the boat to soak up all the vitamin D the bright sun had to offer while enjoying the view. I always been able to handle the dosage of the edibles I got from my weed man, but whatever Brielle had gotten a hold of was some next level shit. I'd never been higher. The captain anchored the yacht a couple miles from an isolated island so that Brielle and Shauna's high asses could start jet skiing. As soon as I closed my mascara-spiked eyes and started to drift off into a light slumber, my phone vibrated against my thigh. I lifted my glasses and looked down to see a number with a Florida area code. A sour look paraded across my face as I quickly hit decline. I knew it was Omar, and he for damn sure wasn't going to bring me down or kill my vibe. His lying, cheating ass could eat a hot, pickled dick as far as I was concerned.

"Bitch ass nigga," I grumbled.

I contemplated tossing my phone into the water and watching it sink to the depths but decided to turn it off instead. I paced to the back of the boat and dropped my phone in the bottom of my bag.

"You good, Cass?" Lauryn asked, approaching me from the left.

I angled my face away from hers. "Mmhm."

"You sure?"

I looked at her and shook my head. "It's Omar. He called."

Her brows creased as she rested her hands on her hour-glass hips. "Did you answer?"

"What you think?" I asked, rolling my eyes.

"I mean, maybe he wants to talk it out. You said he just up and left with no explanation. I'm not saying you gotta take his foul ass back, but maybe you should hear him out."

I sighed, knowing she wouldn't be saying that if she knew the truth. "Okay, listen. What I'm about to tell you, you cannot repeat to any fuckin' body. Not Donovan, and definitely not Shauna or Bri, okay?"

"Um, okay. What the fuck are you about to tell me, Cass? And do I need a shot before it hits my ears?" she questioned.

"Yeah, go ahead and pour one for both of us," I told her.

"Aight, let's go sit down," she said. "I'm baking under this sun."

I nodded, feeling my own skin sizzling under the sun's rays. Once we were seated and shots were poured, I spoke up. "So, um about Omar and me…he didn't exactly just up and leave…"

"Well, bitch, I knew that!"

My face clouded with embarrassment. "How?" I asked.

"Um, because that's some weird ass shit. I just thought that you would tell me when you were ready, and I guess now you are."

As my best friend and blood, Lauryn knew me like I knew the back of my own hand. I was famous for putting off difficult conversations or making difficult decisions for as long as I possibly could. "He cheated on me, Lauryn. Me! And not only did he cheat, but he's having a—a baby with the bitch!"

Lauryn's almond shaped chestnut eyes widened as her eyebrows jutted in surprise. "Oh shit, Cass."

"I was so fuckin' embarrassed about it that I just couldn't tell anyone. I didn't want anybody to know. I just—I did a lot for that mothafucka, you know?"

"Oh, girl. I know. You sure love a good project. I've told you that before. Wouldn't be me."

"I'm a Libra, and I want to see the good in damn near everybody. It's like my only downfall," I admitted.

Lauryn smacked her bow-shaped lips. "It's not but continue."

I huffed. "I just thought it would pay off in the end, you know? I spent the last eighteen months of my life grooming a nigga for the next bitch. Well, not even. The bitch he cheated on me with is his fuckin' ex!" I announced, dropping the next bomb.

Lauryn turned up her lips while shaking her head. "Girl, fuck him! Fuck him for life! You just need a nigga to match or exceed what you bring to the table, and that's not just money. You just haven't found the yin to your yang yet, that's all. But he's out there, I promise."

"What y'all talking about?" Shauna asked, making her way over to us and plopping her mocha-colored body down beside Lauryn.

I cut Lauryn a quick look, and she shook her head. "Girl, niggas. Wait, what happened to the jet skis?" she answered, trying to change the subject.

"Bitch, Brielle's high ass got out there and realized she couldn't swim and started crying," Shauna announced before bubbling over with laughter.

Lauryn's eyes crinkled with laughter. "I swear she's a trip."

"Where is she now?" I inquired.

She pointed her white-painted nails toward the lower level. "In the bathroom. She's okay."

"Oh okay."

"So, what about niggas?" Shauna asked, returning to the previous topic.

"Okay, okay. I got a question and all y'all gotta answer," Lauryn declared.

"What did I miss?" Brielle asked, walking up on the three of us.

"Girl, you okay?" I asked, noticing her puffy, red eyes. I couldn't tell if it was because she was high or if it was from her meltdown in the water.

Brielle bobbed her head, before running her fingers through her blonde box braids. "Yeah, girl. I'm good."

"What happened out there?" Lauryn asked, giggling all over again.

"Bitch, I don't know why I thought I was the lil' fuckin' mermaid or some shit. I got out on that jet ski shit and freaked the fuck out. I said ah hell no, get me back on solid ground, mothafucka!"

The four of us roared with laughter. "See? This is why I love you. You're hilarious!" I told her, flexing my stomach muscles from giggling so hard.

"What can I say? My life is a film," Brielle proclaimed. "But, c'mon, what did I miss? Tell me."

Shauna spoke up and said, "Lauryn was about to ask a question and said we all have to answer."

"Go ahead and ask it. I'm ready," Brielle told Lauryn.

"Okay, so if you could build the perfect nigga, what would your top three must-have traits? And Cassidy has to go first because I asked her this shit once before, and she dodged me."

"Honesty," I blurted out.

"Mmm, yes. I can't stand a lying ass nigga," Shauna chimed in.

"Um, and he's got to bring some level of success to the table. A nigga can't expect me to bring the table and the chairs and put the food on it too," I added.

"Mmm, preach!" Shauna boasted before turning the bottle of tequila up to her lips.

"And a third one…I mean, he gotta look good, right? So yeah, those are my three. I want an honest, successful, good-lookin' nigga," I broadcasted, secretly hoping the universe heard me and delivered. I wasn't ashamed to admit I was big on appearance. I loved a sexy ass nigga.

Lauryn burst out laughing, her white teeth glistened just as brightly as her coppery-brown skin. "Well, good luck with that shit, boo."

I sucked my teeth. "What's the point of doing this if you gon' poke holes all in my shit?"

She chuckled. "I'm just saying. If you find one, that nigga is a unicorn. If he's good-lookin, that mean he broke. If he successful and he look good, then you know that mothafucka is a liar! That's all I'm saying!"

"I hate to agree, but…she right," Brielle agreed, propping up her pink-painted toes on the edge of the table.

"Right as fuck!" Shauna added, flashing her wide-gapped smile.

I sucked my teeth before my eyes crimped in laughter. "Ugh, shut up! Guess I gotta find me an honest, ugly nigga, but I don't know if I can do it. Aesthetics matter, bitch."

"Shit, he still might be broke anyway." Lauryn snickered.

"What about the rest of y'all? All y'all got niggas except for me.

What are three traits your men have that you absolutely love or you wish they had?" I asked, flipping the question on them.

Shauna spoke up. "I'll go first—I'll say I love a man that can use his imagination. Like, give me a nigga with a brain, a good one at that. That's Trey up and down. It's probably my favorite thing about him aside from the D." She winked.

Laughter filled the open vessel once again, bellowing above the speaker. "Ain't nothing wrong with that. If you would've told me I had four traits, a big dick would've been number four," I affirmed.

"Shit, it should really be number one, but I'm just saying." Lauryn shrugged, shaking her honey brown faux goddess locs from side to side.

I turned my attention to Lauryn and Brielle. "C'mon, Brielle, Lauryn? What about y'all? Answer the question!"

"Yeah, I did!" Shauna said.

"Fine, I'll go next," Brielle stated. "Um, I'll say off the top of my head, and don't judge me because y'all already know I'm fucked-up, and I don't even know if it's noon yet, but I love a nigga who is in touch with his feminine side. And I ain't talkin' on no bitch shit, but just someone who can be gentle and compassionate. I love that shit."

"Girl, it sound like all a nigga gotta do is recite you a haiku and you give up the pussy," Lauryn joked.

Snickers bubbled through our mouths, including Brielle's. "Shut up!"

"I'm the complete opposite! Give me a nigga that's gon' dog this pussy out, okay? I don't want no hugs and kisses all the time, I just want a tall, hard-working, strong ass, pussy slaying nigga!" Lauryn declared.

"Amen to that!" I said, giving her a high-five.

"So, what you saying is Donovan's baldheaded, light-skinned ass be havin' you crawlin' up the walls every night, huh?" Shauna asked Lauryn.

"You muh'fuckin' right," Lauryn boasted. "And you leave my bald-headed, fine ass nigga alone," she mocked.

I shrugged. "Y'all lucky y'all all got somebody because there's really nothing out here. Not that I'm looking, but I'm just saying."

"So things are done, done with you and Omar?" Brielle asked.

I bobbed my head. "Stick a fork in that shit."

"So, what happened with that?" Brielle asked.

"Yeah, I don't think I ever got the full story either," Shauna said, eyeing me and bunching her arms up against her size DD-chest.

I shook my head. "There's literally nothing to tell. One day shit was good and the next day it wasn't. He packed his shit and he left, and I haven't heard from him since," I told them.

Shauna and Brielle looked at each other, silently trying to figure out which one was going to call me out on my bullshit. Instead, they turned back to me and shook their heads.

"Niggas," Shauna said, crossing her elongated legs.

"Mmm, you should've been left that nigga. He was probably gay anyway. Where was he from again? Georgia?" Brielle quizzed.

"Guess I'm loyal to a fault. And no. He's from Florida," I corrected her.

Brielle smacked her rose pink lips. "Mmm, yeah, no. You need you a nigga that's born and bred on the West Coast. No more East Coast niggas for you, okay?"

"How are things going with you and Hendrix?" Lauryn blurted out, throwing me for a loop.

Fuck, I thought. Just when I thought I'd made it through the entire boat ride scot free, she brought him up. I couldn't dare tell them about the embarrassing moment I'd had with him the day prior. We hadn't said more than a couple words to each other since his sly remark.

That's the second time this week you've blamed me for getting you wet.

I shook my head, trying to push his voice out of my head long enough to figure out a response that wouldn't prompt more questions from my nosey ass friends. "There's nothing going on. He stays on his side, and I stay on mine. End of story."

Shauna tilted her head while eyeing me. "Mmm, you sound angry."

Brielle chimed in. "I'd have to agree with Shauna's statement. You sitting over there with a million-dollar dick under the same roof as you and you mad? Girl, you crazy as hell!"

"Crazy as fuck!" Shauna added before high-fiving Brielle and laughing.

"I heard his dick so big, bitches call him *The Womb Raider*. But as far as we know, no kids, right?" Brielle quizzed, spilling and fishing for the tea at the same time.

"Nope, no kids," Lauryn confirmed.

"So, that's even more of a plus. No baby mama drama!"

"You mean no NBA baby mama drama. You know them bitches are extra as fuck. Don't act like you ain't never watch *Basketball Wives*!" Shauna stated.

"First of all, I don't care about what he's got between his legs or if he's got some kids because I just got rid of one nigga. What makes y'all think I want to deal with another one?" I quizzed them.

"Everybody ain't healthy for you, girl. As much as it sucks, it's the reality of the shit. But Hendrix...he could be the antidote. That's all I'm saying. Besides, you know you used to like that boy," Lauryn said in a convincing voice.

I shot up to my feet. "Okay, first of all, everybody and they mama used to like that boy. The tea is, I'm the only one who was smart enough not to fall for his shit."

"Girl, sit your self-righteous ass down! I may be fucked-up, but I recall you saying you wanted an honest, fine ass, successful nigga, right? I don't know if the mothafucka is honest, but he can ball and he look good doing it," Brielle declared, using my own words against me.

I plopped down in my seat and folded my arms across my chest. They didn't know how right they were. I *was* living under the same roof with a *big ass* million-dollar dick. Little did they know, thoughts of him had been playing on mute in the back of my mind since my eyes collided with his on the plane. Then after seeing what the good Lord had blessed him with, I'd already fucked him every which way to Sunday in my mind. The dick looked too damn good not to fantasize about. I'd rehearsed what I'd do to him over and over again until I practically had it down to a science.

Lauryn gasped. "Oh shit, I've got an idea!"

I shook my head. "Whatever it is, no."

"I need you to keep an open mind, Cass."

"What is it?" I asked, rolling my disapproving eyes.

"We're going out later tonight, right? You should invite him to come out with us!"

A scoff slipped past my lips. "What? No. Hell no! Why?"

"It would be good to see him! It's not like I'm around when him and Mark ever link up. And girl, you know Donovan is a big fan."

Shauna bobbed her head. "Hell yeah, Trey is too."

"So not only do I have to suffer in my villa, but now you're asking me to suffer through an entire outing with him just so y'all men can get their fangirl on?"

"Please? It is my birthday, remember?" Lauryn reminded me.

Brielle chimed in, "I mean, my nigga ain't a big basketball fan, but honestly, I just want him to come so I can watch you squirm." She chuckled, rubbing her butterscotch-colored shoulder against mine.

I kissed my teeth. "Whatever. I'll ask, but I ain't making no promises. And if the nigga says no, I'm not begging his ass."

"That's all I'm asking," Lauryn agreed.

"Can we be done with nigga talk now and get back to these shots and fun shit?" I asked, before pouring myself another shot.

"Pour another round, then!" Brielle cheered.

ten

. . .

HENDRIX

The loud growling of my stomach prompted me to step out of my room for a mid-afternoon trip to the kitchen. As soon as I popped around the corner, I saw Cassidy staring into the open refrigerator.

"Yo, you good?" I asked, watching her minimal gestures.

Deep in thought, she stood frozen, staring into the fridge with her ass hanging out of the bottom of her snow-white bikini bottom. I instantly sunk my teeth into my bottom lip, careful not to let anything obscene fall off my lips. Cassidy turned to face me, her eyes hazed from whatever she'd ingested.

"I'm so fuckin' thirsty, but I can't find anything to drink."

My eyes narrowed as my neck cocked to the side. "You high?"

Her cat-shaped eyes widened. "Oh shit, you can tell?"

I roared with laughter. Her ass was fucked-up. "What the fuck did you do today?"

"Brielle had a weed brownie," she confessed, "and I may have eaten some of said weed brownie on a boat...and washed it down with a few shots of tequila."

I chuckled. She was cute when she was fucked-up. Definitely more tolerable. "Oh shit, y'all was lit. I ain't know your girl was out here."

"Yeah, it's Lauryn's birthday."

"Lauryn? Like Mark's sister?"

"Yeah, so all my girls are here with they niggas."

"Word? And where your nigga at?" I inquired.

"Why I gotta have a nigga to come on vacation?"

"You don't, I'm just saying you don't strike me as the type to vacation alone, that's all."

She rolled her eyes. "It's a long story, but all you need to know is I ain't got one to be worried about."

I bobbed my head. "Mmm, it makes sense now."

Her feathery eyelashes fluttered in annoyance. "What?"

"That's why you were so mad when I got here. You were supposed to be here with another nigga, huh?"

Her brows knotted. "I'm too fucked-up for this. Just mind your business, nigga."

I chuckled at her fine flustered ass. "Yeah, aight. You ain't gotta admit it, it's cool."

"Can you just shut up and help me?"

"Help you with what?"

"Listen, I—I can't be this fucked-up for the rest of the day. We're supposed to be going out tonight."

"Your lightweight ass need to get some food in you to soak all that shit up and then take a long ass nap," I advised. "If you do that, you'll be straight."

"Can you order me something?"

"I was coming in here to order something for myself, so I got you. You go on and take your ass in the room."

"Okay, thanks," she said, turning to leave and then doing a 180-degree turn. "Oh, before I forget, Lauryn wanted me to tell you to come out to the club tonight with everybody if you want, but no pressure."

"I wasn't gon' do shit but chill anyway, so as long as it's lowkey that's cool. I'll come."

When the food arrived, I took it over to her room and knocked on her door. "Cassidy? Aye, yo, Cass? Food is here."

After waiting a few seconds for a response, I opened the door to see her sprawled out across her bed still in her bikini, with all that ass hanging out the bottom. For a minute, I debated on whether to cover her up or enjoy the view. Instead, I walked over to her gently shook her shoulder.

"Yo, Cassidy. Your food is here. Where you want me to leave it?"

Her hazy eyes opened at the sound of my voice. "What did you get me?"

"I ordered you the greasiest shit I could find on the menu. You wanna sit up and eat it now or you want me to put it off to the side somewhere?" I asked.

"Mmm, feed me," she mumbled as the shadow of her eyelashes swept against her cheeks.

"What?"

"Feed me. Please?" she asked, softening her tone.

"I take it you don't get fucked-up too often."

"I'm a security software engineer, what do you think?" She chuckled, pushing hair out of her face.

I removed the cover from her food and grabbed a crispy French fry and held it up to her lips. She quickly chomped it down as if it was the best thing since sliced bread. I took a seat on the edge of her bed while she managed to sit up and elevate herself with a few pillows.

"We both know what I did after high school, but what about you?" I asked, serving up a few more fries and a bottle of water.

After sucking down half a bottle of water, she replied, "I got my degree in computer science and minored in finance. From there, I went on to an internship at Google and then landed an entry level job in Silicon Valley at Apple. I worked there for two years and just recently found a home with Capital One."

My brows lifted. "Wow, congrats."

"Thanks."

"What made you get into computers?"

"In school, my favorite subject was always math, and when you couple that with careers that are going to make you the big bucks, it was kind of a no-brainer."

"So, you must be good with crunching numbers and shit."

"It's more than being good at numbers. You have to have the certifications to make the real money. I'm talking, IAT, SSCP, CISSP—"

I threw my hands up in the air. "Okay, chill. It just sound like you throwin' the alphabet at me right now. I get it, you gotta be smart. You've always been that."

She shrugged before tossing a few more fries in her mouth. "I know."

I shot her a disapproving glance. "Damn, you can't even take a compliment from a nigga."

She held her hands out in protest. "No, I—I didn't mean it like that. What I meant to say was—"

"Thank you?" I said, cutting her off at the pass.

She sighed. "Yeah."

"You got it from here? I'm about to eat my own shit before it gets cold," I asked, passing her the plate of fries and wings. If she was coherent enough to talk, she was coherent enough to feed her damn self.

"Yeah, I do."

"Aight, cool. I'll see you later."

"Hendrix, wait!" she called out.

My neck turned back in the direction of her voice. "Yeah?"

"Thank you…"

I bobbed my head. "You're more than welcome."

eleven

. . .

CASSIDY

I woke up hours later, feeling like a new woman. We'd gotten fucked-up so early in the day that when I woke up that evening, I felt like it was the next day. After sitting up slowly, I stretched and drew in the lingering scent of warm, blue skies and fields of amber from Hendrix's cologne against my comforter. After stepping out of the shower and doing my hair and makeup for the night, I decided on a short, dusty blue silk dress and strappy four-inch black heels. With my cell turned back on, ignoring Omar's calls for the umpteenth time had me fighting the urge to get fucked-up all over again.

We stepped into the club and were immediately greeted with blue, pink, and purple neon-hued strobe lights. The DJ was on the mic hyping up the crowd that was packed shoulder to shoulder on the dance floor. As soon as word got around that a professional NBA player was in the building, we were all quickly rushed to a private VIP section. Soon, our section was flooded with bottles of Casa Migos, Cîroc, and Hennessy, causing my girls and their men to cheese from ear to ear.

"Lauryn, you're the smartest bitch alive," Shauna said, nudging her.

"I know, right." Lauryn giggled.

"Order anything y'all want on me," Hendrix announced.

"Hell yeah! Thank you, Hendrix! I'ma fuck up all the Hennessy in this bitch just for you!" Brielle cheered.

As the hours passed, I couldn't help but find my eyes perched on him from wherever he was. It was clear he had all my attention. When the DJ started spinning *Essence* by WizKid and Tems, my body moved as effortlessly as a flag in the wind. I began twerking in my seat with one hand in the air and swaying my head from side to side. The bold, recognizable scent I'd spent time inhaling earlier wafted past my nostrils, indicating he was near. My eyes popped open just in time to see him take his place in front of me with an outstretched hand.

"I know you ain't gon' sit on all that ass all night. Go on and shake somethin' for a nigga, Cass." *There he was with that Cass shit again.* I admired the way my name rolled off his lips with ease.

"Is that your way of asking me to dance?" I chuckled.

I looked around at all my girls who were in their own zones with their men and then back at Hendrix, whose eyes pointed upward toward the dance floor. The cute, but uncomfortable heels I wore had my dogs barking and as much as I wanted to sit and look cute, I wasn't about to pass up a chance to shamelessly brush up against all he had to offer. I took his hand and stood to my feet as his fingers appeared around my waist. I began winding my hips to the beat as my ass grated against his dick. With my waist encircled by his grasp, his hands guided my body like a snake charmer.

"Bust it open for a nigga," his deep-throated voice hummed against my ear.

As much as I wanted to ask, *now or later*? I refrained and continued to grind my body against his for the remainder of the song.

When the mix went from one song to the next and I found myself still caged in between his muscular arms, I continued to dance as if we were the only two people in the vicinity. It was clear the liquor or my true feelings had taken over and before I knew it, his beautiful pink lips were attached to mine, and my hands were tangled in his beard in the middle of the VIP section.

Hendrix pulled his lips away from mine before flashing a subtle smile. I stood there, stalled in awe like a moth to a flame. The fuse had been lit. Before I could even wrap my head around what happened, my phone vibrated violently in my left hand.

"I, uh—excuse me," I said before turning to walk out.

I darted out of the club, trying to find a quiet place to slow down my racing heartbeat and thoughts. Omar had been calling at least twice an hour all day. Even after cutting my phone off for hours at a time, he'd resorted to leaving multiple voicemails. My heart had come to a fork in the road. As much as I knew I needed to leave him right where he was, I was torn between my heart saying answer and my mind rebelling against it. Before I had time to weigh the pros and cons, the phone stopped vibrating. The universe had made the decision for me. Just when I thought I could exhale, the vibrations started up again. Acting off alcoholic impulse and annoyance, I hit accept and put the phone up to my ear.

"So, that's what we've resorted to? Calling me from multiple numbers back-to-back all day long?" I quizzed.

"What else was I supposed to do, Cass? You blocked me on everything," Omar said on the other end. The sound of his voice instantly coated my skin in goosebumps.

"You damn right I did, and I'm about to block this number next. We don't have anything to talk about."

"We both know that's not true," he disagreed.

I scoffed. "Oh, but it is."

"Listen, Cass. I—I just need you to hear me out, okay? That's all I'm asking for."

I huffed. "Please don't waste my time with this shit."

"I just need to tell you that I'm sorry."

I sucked my sparkling white teeth, trying to drown out his empty ass apology. You apologize when you step on someone's foot or say something offensive. He'd went off and procreated with a bitch he told me he couldn't stand, and he thought a simple *I'm sorry* was going to make up for that? His mistake would soon have a birthdate. We were far from cards, flowers, and apologies now.

"What is it about the words *we have nothing to discuss* that you don't understand? I said what I said, Omar."

"I let you down, and I'm sorry for that, Cass. Okay? I fucked up, and I know that. I—I just feel like I still want this."

An annoyed grunt slipped past my lips. "Nigga, have you lost your fuckin' mind?"

"Isn't the love we have for each other enough to make you want to find a way to make this work between us? We can do counseling or anything."

My lips curled with anger. "Counseling that I'd have to front the bill for, Omar? The problem with our entire relationship was that I loved you more than you could ever love me. You let me come in last to the job that *I* got *you*, your wants, your needs, and even your ex. My only mistake in this entire waste of a relationship was making you a priority when I was nothing but a second thought to your ass!"

"I didn't mean for any of this to happen."

"The baby or the fucking? Which one? I'd like some clarity."

"Cassidy, I—"

"No, fuck you, Omar! You were the one that decided you ain't want this shit no more the moment you stuck your dick inside that bitch. And when you found out she was pregnant, what did you do? You chose to hide it from me until just when you were about to pack your shit and have your fuckin' mail forwarded to Florida! Now, you wanna come back into my life with the I'm sorry bullshit, and I'm tellin' you to stay where the fuck you at!"

I wanted to emasculate him and make him feel as small as an atom. It was best to leave things where they were. The second I heard him sob through the receiver, I ended the call. I was back where I started, with my guard up and my heart under wraps. I was beyond tired of synthetic love. He could ride off into the fuckin' sunset and have rainbows and unicorn sprinkles shoot out of his asshole with that pregnant bitch as far as I was concerned. I quickly swiped away angry tears and tried my best to regain my composure by counting backwards from twenty. One call from him and his ass had me right back in my feelings and raging all over again. Instead of going back inside the club, I went back to the villa to sulk in peace.

———

Twenty minutes later, I heard a knock on my door. "Yeah?" I called out.

"Everything good?" Hendrix asked.

My shoulders locked up. I'd been so caught up with a surprise second helping of bullshit from Omar that I hadn't even gotten the chance to dissect the brief kiss that Hendrix and I shared in the club. My lips tingled with passion at the thought of it.

"The way you ran up outta there so fast, I figured I should come check on you," he continued.

"Uh, yeah. I'm good. I'm fine."

"You sure?"

"Yeah," I said, resting my palm against the cold door.

"Then, open the door and let me see you."

My heart danced with butterflies as I quickly got in front of a mirror to confirm what my eyes already knew. I looked a mess. Mascara was smeared underneath my glossy-teared eyes, and both my makeup and edges were sweated out. "I, uh—"

"Open the door," he demanded.

His paralyzing, baritone voice set my lungs on fire as I walked back over to the door and obliged him. The second his eyes pinned on mine; I was completely disarmed. There was no need in letting my heart get in the way of what my head already knew. If he could make me feel like I was breathing underwater with just a look, I wouldn't be able to handle anything else he had to offer. He was a hazard to my health.

"You got some bad news or somethin'?"

"Why do you ask?"

"I saw you pacing back and forth outside the club on your phone. By the time I came out to check on you, you were gone."

I shook my head, putting his suspicions to rest. "No. I was uh, on the phone with my ex."

He bobbed his head before running his hand down his beard. "Mmm, I figured it was nigga problems."

My teeth clicked together with an attitude, shifting the energy in the room from somber to defensive. "Why you say it like that?"

"I'm a smart nigga, Cass. Plus, you not as lowkey with your feeling as you think you are. More importantly, I know a bad bitch when I see one, so why you lettin' a nigga treat you like you anything but?"

I wrinkled my nose at him. "You don't even know what he did."

"It don't matter. The nigga ain't here, right? So, he old news in my book," he said, stepping inside my room and making himself comfortable at the foot of my messy bed.

I massaged my stiff neck with my index finger before pushing a sigh past my lips. "You don't get it. I've always had to prove myself. Whether it's in the boardroom or the bedroom. Shit is different for people like you. There are people lined up waiting to give you anything you want. Whereas somebody like me has to beg and fight for a nigga to treat me right and to be seen."

"I've always seen you," he admitted.

My drifting eyes flashed up to meet his. "What did you just say?"

"You heard me."

My head shook in protest. "No, I don't think I did."

"The way you glow whenever you talk about something you're passionate about, or the sexy way you move your body to music, the way your eyes glisten when you're lost in thought. You don't even know you're the fuckin' center of attention to every nigga within a few feet of your presence. I see everything about you. And if I'm bein' honest, I always have."

I could feel my cheeks burning. As bad as I wanted to sink into the floor, I couldn't move. A sudden paralysis overcame me from the roots of my scalp to the soles of my feet. His words had rendered a bitch completely speechless.

"I—I don't know what to say... I don't think I've ever really been seen before...by anyone," I acknowledged.

"Well, I'll say this, you got all my attention," he said, biting down on his sexy ass bottom lip.

I felt a knot as large as a melon lodged in my throat. I was usually quick on my feet but his confession had me off balance. Had I suddenly been transported to an alternate universe where Hendrix and I actually enjoyed one another's company?

I folded my arms across my chest. "You say all of that, yet you were horrible to me growing up, Hendrix."

"Let me make it up to you. You wanna hug it out?" he joked before walking over and pulling me into his arms.

I giggled. "Boy, get your ass off me!"

I only put up a minimal fight before melting into his chest. My heart drummed at a million beats per minute as I tried to steady my breathing. *Don't lose your shit, Cass. Don't lose your fuckin' shit*, I repeated over and over in my mind.

"But for the record, your ass was never nothin' nice to me either," he replied.

"Rightfully, so. You were and still are, an asshole when you wanna be."

He shrugged his broad shoulders. "I'll take that."

I flashed him a gentle smile. "Thank you, Hendrix."

"For what?"

"For checking on me and delivering me from my self-pitying bullshit."

"I figured you delivered me from mine, so I should at least return the favor. That nigga don't deserve you, so ain't no need in wasting another tear on 'em."

"On period!"

He chuckled. "On period. So, what you about to do? Go to sleep?"

I shook my head. "I was actually thinking about taking a walk on the beach. You know, to clear my head."

"You want some company? I could kick it with you if you not tired of me already."

The remaining liquor in my system made me nod with a quickness. "Sure."

My misery had acquired his company, and I was in no way ready to let go. Never in my wildest dreams would I have pictured myself walking on the beach at two o'clock in the morning and revealing my demons to someone I usually loathed on any given day. Emotionally, I was spiraling out of control, and I had no way of stopping it. And yet, there I was, staring into his Hennessy brown eyes as he listened to me talk about my shitty love life. The depths of his waves shimmered underneath the yellow moonlight. I couldn't help but stare at him because he was just *that* fine.

"You know, I thought this week was going to be a bust, but uh, I... I'll admit, I'm enjoying my time here...with you," I told him.

"You not so bad yourself once I was able to knock that glacier-sized chip off your shoulder."

I frowned. "I didn't have a—" He cut his eyes at me, silently calling me out on my bullshit. "Okay, fine. Yes. I had a big ass chip on my shoulder, but now you know why. You know I didn't even have the balls to tell Lauryn the truth at first? I just told her today and told everybody else that he up and left with no explanation because in some sick, twisted ass way, I wish that's what would've really happened."

"Why?"

"Honestly?" I asked.

"That's the only way I want you to give it to me."

"I can't take the embarrassment and everybody forming their opinions and feeling sorry for me. I'm not a charity case, you know?"

He bobbed his head. "I get it. Trust me, I do."

"It's just, when I love, I love hard. And it always bites me in the ass. It may not be right away, but it always does."

"There's nothing wrong with loving hard. That's what you supposed to do."

"I've never had a problem falling in love, I just don't need a nigga pretending that he give a fuck about me or my well-being when he don't. And because of that right there, there are a lot of people and things that'll never get a second of my time again, him included."

"I'ma let you in on a little secret. Niggas don't fuckin' abandon the heart of someone they truly love, okay? They only abandon the people they were using."

I swallowed hard. His words hit me like a fuckin' Mack truck. "Damn," I mumbled, choking back tears. "I'm a complicated ass puzzle. I'm aware that I'm probably missing a few pieces that will never be found, too. Sometimes, I just think maybe I'm better off by myself."

"You just gotta find the nigga who brings your missing pieces to the table, that's all."

My eyes drifted across his face in surprise. "When the fuck did you get so wise?"

"I've always known this. If you bothered to talk to me, then maybe you'd know."

I rolled my eyes. "That goes both ways, but okay."

"You know one thing I've learned about you?"

"What's that?"

"You always have to be right."

I shot him a disapproving brow. "No, I don't."

"Yes, you do. Even right now, you're trying to argue with me about why you should be right when you should really just fuckin' listen. If you just kept that pretty ass mouth shut and listened half as much as you talked, your hardheaded ass might learn something."

His remark about my mouth made me bring my fingers to my lips before I let out a sharp exhale. I knew I had trouble admitting my faults, but who didn't? "Can you not come at my neck right now?" I asked.

"I'm not. I'm just being honest with you. You ain't never had a real nigga and it shows, but don't worry. All that's about to change."

I twisted my neck in his direction as we approached our villa and stepped inside. "You care to elaborate on what that means?"

He turned his body to mine, causing me to press my back against the door. "It means I know what you need."

"And what's that?" I asked, arching a questioning brow with my head cocked to the side.

His hands absorbed my hips as he leaned into my ear. "Good dick and advice," he said, leaning down to let his lips gently dominate mine. "Sleep well, Cassidy."

He escaped to his room, leaving me with my mouth gaped open and a pair of soaked panties. Just before the sun started to peak through the dark sky, I drifted off to sleep with thoughts of Hendrix dancing through my head. Maybe his fine ass wasn't so bad after all.

twelve

. . .

Day Five

CASSIDY

Hendrix and I fused our lips roughly against each other, and he lifted my dress over my thighs. His wandering hands naturally found the curve of my hips and rested there. He pressed his dick against me, and I felt it growing harder by the minute.

"I want you to drain it," he whispered against my lips.

I protested with the shake of my head. "Hendrix, we can't…"

He pressed his thumb against my clit, and my hips gaped open like the iPhone Touch I.D. granting him instant access to the treasure between my thighs.

"Please, stop…this — this isn't right," I mumbled while letting him slip my lace panties to the side. My mouth said one thing, but my body said another. It was clear that my mind and dripping wet pussy weren't on the same page.

"Tell me it's mine, Cass," he decreed, driving his fingers into the depths of my tightness.

"Stop before I cum," I moaned.

He leaned in to place wispy kiss my neck. "I'll stop when you tell me it's mine."

"It's yours!" I cried out as he finger-fucked me to my peak. "It's all fuckin' yours."

Hendrix's expressive eyes closed in on mine as he slowly pulled his sticky fingers away and sucked the sweetness of my juices off them. "That's what I like to hear," he said before bending down to kiss me.

My sweat-drenched body shot up in my bed as my heart drummed in my chest. My bugged-out eyes quickly scanned the room to confirm that I was alone and that everything I'd experienced had only occurred in my wildest dreams. That nigga had just made me cum in my sleep without laying a finger on me.

"Fuck!" I groaned, flopping my head back against the plush bed pillow.

I swept a few braids out of my face and tried to settle my thoughts. I was so horny, I felt like my brain was spinning on its axis. He said *good dick and advice* was what I needed. He'd already given up the advice, and my body was more than ready for the dick. In an effort to cool the blazing thoughts in my head, I swiped up my vibrator and hit the shower to take the edge off.

Thirty minutes later, I emerged from the bathroom looking and feeling as fresh as a daisy. The moment I decided to venture out of my room and into the common areas, I saw a shirtless Hendrix coming in from the pool terrace. My eyes outlined his washboard-tight stomach before speaking up.

"H—hey," I greeted him while squeezing my thighs together.

"Hey, yourself."

"What were you about to do?" I probed.

"Well, I was going to go outside and do a couple laps in the pool, but it looks like it's about to storm."

His statement made me turn my eyes to the nearest window. Patches of dark clouds covered the sky, blocking out all light from the sun. I'd been too preoccupied with my own dark desires to even notice the change in the weather.

"You think it's gonna be a quick shower or an all-day thing?"

"I checked the weather and it's supposed to go all day, storms and all that."

I lowered my head. "Damn, I wanted to go check out some of the local shops today, but it looks like I'm going to be kicking it here."

"You talk to your girls?"

I lifted my shoulders in a slight shrug. "Nah, I'm not even gon' bother. If the weather is like this, then I already know all them hoes is booed up."

"Oh, so I see we both gon' be in the house bored."

"Well, in that case, do you wanna watch a movie or somethin'?"

"Yeah, turn on the TV and see what they got that's good," he suggested, "and you better not pick no whack ass shit either."

I sucked my teeth. "Whatever. And while I'm doing that, you can order us some breakfast."

"That's cool. I was just about to make myself some coffee. You want one?"

"Coffee sounds good."

"How do you take it?" he inquired, raising his eyebrow in interest.

My cheeks burned hot. "Excuse me?"

He smirked. "How do you take your coffee, Cassidy?"

I swallowed loudly. "Oh, uh two sugars, two creams. You?"

"Black. I don't do all the extra sugars and shit."

"Oh, I forgot you gotta keep that body right," I teased.

"You look like you know a thing or two about that yourself."

I chewed the inside of my cheek, trying to prevent a smirk from appearing across my face. "Was that your way of complimenting me?" I quizzed while making my way into the living room to turn on the TV.

"Maybe," he baited me.

I clicked on the movie streaming app and typed in letters until *The Wood* showed up. The pregnant thunder clouds soon gave way to billions of dime-sized raindrops just as I tapped play.

"Shit, it don't look like we gon' be gettin' food delivered anytime soon," Hendrix announced, listening to the rumble of the downpour around us.

He made his way around to the couch and handed me a steaming hot coffee mug as I curled my feet underneath me. A few minutes into the movie, my eyes traveled over to Hendrix whose torso was comfortably outstretched across the couch. As ceaseless rain pelted from the sky, we laid lazily across the oversized couch cushions indulging in our favorite movie. We shared a common laugh when young Mike tried to teach himself how to dance and when him and his boys found themselves caught in the middle of a convenience store robbery on the way to the dance.

———

I woke up to the savory smells of food wafting past my nose without even realizing the cloudburst of rain from the Caribbean storm had ushered me off to sleep. Intrigued by the smell, I lazily made my way into the kitchen.

"What smells so good in here?"

"I just finished throwing down in this mothafucka. That's what smells so good in here," he boasted.

I rolled my eyes. "Boy, please."

"C'mon, sit down. Let's eat."

I followed him into the dining room where all the food was already plated and laid out to perfection. We had lobster bisque and Caesar salad to start. Followed by seafood pasta with lobster sauce, and chocolate truffle cake topped with vanilla bean ice cream for dessert.

"Wow," I said, clanking my chocolate-stained spoon on the side of the plate, "this was amazing."

"Hell yeah."

"You uh, really put it down. All this food and not one dirty dish," I teased.

He rolled his tongue against his teeth before smiling. "Yeah, uh about that. I may have had a private chef prepare all this shit and deliver it to us, but I did reheat it. That's what had it smellin' so good."

I grinned as a soft chuckle whipped past my lips. "I know, but I wasn't gon call you out. I knew you didn't know your way around the kitchen that damn good, but it was a nice gesture," I said, ushering a coy shrug.

"Oh, so I was caught from the beginning, huh?"

"Yeah, you were."

"You cook?" he asked.

I shook my head. "Barely. I make the essentials, trust me. Ramen, spaghetti, fried chicken and cereal," I confessed as my shoulders silently shook with laughter.

"Ah, hell!" he teased.

A wide grin spread across my face. Being around Hendrix felt new and fresh like the reset button I needed. I'd gone from a permanent scowl to frowns to all thirty-two teeth-showing smiles. "Shut up! Do you cook?"

"I got a couple signature dishes."

"Oh yeah? Like what?"

"I've perfected a good grilled salmon, and my mama's mac and cheese recipe."

"Shit, at least your mom gave you something useful. All I got was constant nagging."

"Word? I always thought you had the perfect lil' family set up."

"I didn't know you noticed, but uh, no—it wasn't. Far from it, actually. Growing up, my mother was the type of person whose love didn't come free. I had to buy it; and not with money, but with things that would make her actually care to admit that I was her daughter. *Stand up straight, don't slouch. Don't grind your teeth. Marry up. Get an education. You're putting on extra weight, go workout. Do something with your hair. No one will ever notice you if you dress like that.*"

"Damn."

"Yeah, so if I wasn't *perfect* then I wasn't her daughter. If I wasn't *winning*, I wasn't her daughter. If I wasn't *number fucking one*, I wasn't her daughter."

"That's crazy."

"After my father died, I put some much-needed distance between me and Inglewood and never looked back."

"Y'all still talk?"

I shrugged. "She calls from time to time, mainly to tell me how I could've done something better from something she saw posted on my Facebook. You know, always criticizing me about something."

"You don't need that type of energy in your life."

"Eh, I'm used to it by now, but that's exactly why I live in San Jose. But at the end of the day, she's still my mother. Ain't nothin' I can do about that."

"I don't give a fuck who she is. That's negative as hell and you don't need that shit. Nobody fuckin' needs that shit. If I was you, I would've been told her about herself."

I was over talking about my mother, so I decided to change the subject. "What about you? How's your family?"

He let out a soft sigh. "Pops is good. He's got about another ten before he's even eligible for parole. Moms is doing good, too. She got her house and her cars and shit like she's always had, so you ain't gon' hear a complaint outta her."

"What did they say about the trade?"

"Pops told me to keep my head up and stay focused on the game. Whereas, Moms don't really give a fuck as long as I'm still doing what I love, and the money is coming in."

I frowned. "Damn."

"Yeah, I know."

"Real talk, this conversation is about to drive me to drink. You want a shot?" I offered.

"Sure."

"Oh, and before I forget, Lauryn invited me to her birthday dinner tomorrow night. I hope that's cool."

"Yeah, no. That's fine."

"You sure? I don't want you to think I'm tryna impede all on your trip and shit."

"It's just a meal, Hendrix. It's fine."

———

A three-course meal and two Shots of D'usse later, I was feeling buzzed and frisky. I paced back and forth between the kitchen and dining room, cleaning off the table and putting our dishes in the sink. Hendrix occupied himself by pouring us a third shot and bringing it over to me.

"Bottoms up," he said.

After downing my shot, I brushed my arm against his at the sink and smiled. "Question."

"Answer," he told me.

"You remember what you told me last night? About you knowing what I needed?"

"Yeah, I do. What about it?"

"Well, you gave the advice. When you gon' give me the dick?" I quizzed with more confidence than initially anticipated. The moment the sentence escaped my lips, I slammed my eyes shut in mortification. *This can't be happening,* I thought to myself. There was no doubt that the sexual chemistry was so thick, it could've smothered us both, but my outburst of honesty caused my body go into complete meltdown mode.

"I don't even know why I just said that," I admitted.

"Because it's what you want."

"Well, is it something you want to give me?"

"I was just waiting on you to give me the green light."

My lips curved upward to a smile as I stepped up and pressed my fluttering chest against his. "Then go," I whispered against his lips as my fingers curled around his dick print.

I stood up on the tips of my toes and slid his wife beater to the side before softly kissing his tattooed shoulder. His eyes cascaded down to mine as he cradled the sides of my face in his hands. What started as a soft, intimate kiss grew more passionate as his back rested against the countertop. Hendrix wrapped his arms around my dainty waist and kissed me deeper. He scooped me up and propped me up on the kitchen island, careful not to break the kiss. His large hands palmed my ass like it had Spalding written across it as he gently pushed me back against the cold, smooth surface.

Pants and shirt, to the left.
Bra and panties, to the right.

Each article of clothing decorated the floor in a telling trail all the way to my bed. My attempt to box him out was a failure. I was on fire for him. Hendrix had my pussy spilling over like a dam at capacity as my flesh anticipated his warm touch. His fingertips skated over my nipples before he sucked on them slowly while his hands roamed all over my body.

I palmed the back of his head, enjoying his kisses from my stomach down to the warmth in between my thighs.

"This is the meal I've been waiting for all day," he whispered before sinking between my legs.

That was it. My pussy was in his possession and there was no such thing as a timeout. My back arched as he pushed my legs toward the heavens and quickly splashed his tongue against my clit. My mouth gaped open in the O-shape as I ran my fingers over his waves.

"Ooooh shit," I cooed.

Heavy breathing and moaning were the only two things I could do as he lapped up my honey like a kitten to warm milk. My eyes popped wide when I heard the vibrating noise and felt the strong pulsating feeling across my clit. *He'd discovered my fuckin' vibrator.*

"Oh! Oh my fuckin'—I, I'm about to fuckin' c—cum!" I screamed.

"Cum in my mouth," he growled.

Hendrix continued to lather my sweet spot with saliva, working in tandem with the vibrator against my clit and two fingers inside me. The instant I reached my peak, I flipped him over onto his back and straddled him. His beard glistened with my cum as we continued to kiss slowly.

"I want all of you," I confessed before inching down to place kisses all over his body.

My fingertips raced over the peaks and valleys of his tattooed skin as I curled my tongue around his nipples and licked each one of his eight abs. Eyes continuing downward, I smiled when I saw his stiff dick waiting for me. It was like seeing the light at the end of the tunnel. I took his Godsend of a dick inside my hand, running it up and down his length before slowly lowering my lips down on it.

"Mmm, shit," he growled, inching down to wrap his hand around a handful of my braids.

He fucked the back of my throat until I gagged and came up for air. I kissed the tip and swirled my tongue over the head before sucking on it. With a combination of hands, tongue, and throat, I continued to pleasure him.

"Goddamn, you about to drain me," he confessed.

I flashed a satisfactory smile. As much as I wanted to suck every fuckin' drop of cum out of him, I needed to know what the dick was about. I'd fantasized about it too long not to.

Hendrix climbed on top of me, holding my body in a passionate embrace. He spread my legs from east to west and inched his ten-inch snake inside me.

"Oh my God!" I cried out, watching his length enter me inch by inch.

I'd finally gotten the thick, long dick I'd been literally dreaming about and it was everything I thought it would be.

"I wanna make that pussy cum tonight. You gonna let me make that pussy cum tonight?" he asked.

"Yes," I moaned, balling the sheets up in my fist.

He smiled as my breasts jiggled underneath his chest. "Mmm, keep moaning for me."

My mouth clung to his as I wrapped him in my thighs. He locked his hand behind my neck and swirled his hips to a melodic rhythm that only our bodies could hear.

"Yes! Go deep!" I squealed.

I clawed my nails over his biceps as he pounded into me, doing push-ups in the pussy. My body trembled with pleasure as I came all over his dick.

"Shit, you see that cum all over my dick? I love that shit. Come here, I wanna fuck that pussy over the balcony," he asserted.

Fresh golden flashes of lightning split the wet sky as Hendrix bent me over the balcony, spread my thighs like butter on toast, and started eating my pussy from behind. I drew in air, holding my breath as he fingered me hard and fast before burying his dick back inside me.

"Mmm, shit!" I groaned.

Hendrix smacked my ass. "Yeah, that's it. Throw that shit back."

"Mmm! Fuck! I'm about to c—cum again!"

I tossed my hair from side to side as he went balls deep inside me. As brutal as it sounded, the multiple, back-spasming orgasms he rained down on me felt heavenly. Hendrix pulled me back into the bedroom and flipped me upside down so that he could eat my pussy standing up. He locked his strong arms around my waist and buried his tongue inside me.

"Oooooh shit, Hendrix! Yesssss!" I screamed, sucking in air through my teeth and popping my pussy against his face.

Moments later, I lathered up his hard dick with fresh spit and jacked him off before we switched into a new position back on the bed.

"You want me to pound that pussy?" he asked, pulling me on top of him and thrusting back inside me.

"Ah shit. Yes!" I cried out.

His sweat-sheened abs flexed as he bucked upwards into me while tugging at my nipples. My neck flew back in ecstasy as the tips of my braids swayed against my ass. Hendrix leaned forward and hooked his tongue around my bouncing nipples as I galloped against him.

"Ooh shit," he groaned, tossing his head back against the headboard. "Yeah, that's it right there. Ride this fuckin' dick."

His grip got tighter as he thrusted harder inside me until we climaxed in unison. Our chests rose and fell rapidly as we crashed against the sticky, wet sheets. I lazily let my head crash against his torso. "Damn." I sighed. "That was—"

"Fuckin' amazing," he answered, completing my sentence.

"I think I want some more…"

"Good, because I've got plans to fuck your beautiful ass all over this fuckin' house tonight," he avowed.

thirteen

. . .

Day Six

HENDRIX

I'd spent the past eight hours buried deep inside Cassidy and being around her had become second nature to me. She had a nigga hooked. We'd gone four rounds back-to-back, and I still hadn't fully decided if I was suffering from a judgment lapse or if Cassidy Stokes was just what the doctor ordered. Whatever it was, the pussy was too damn good to have any regrets the morning after.

I glanced down at the Gucci watch adorning my wrist. "How much longer are you going to take getting ready!" I yelled at Cassidy, who had barricaded herself inside the bathroom for the past hour.

"You can't rush perfection," she replied.

I smirked and decided to take a few puffs of my cigar and fix myself a drink while I waited. The longer she made me wait, the more impatient I got. I debated on whether to barge back inside her room and drag her to Lauryn's birthday dinner kicking and screaming. Just as I finished my drink and sat the brandy glass on the countertop, I heard the clicking of heels behind me. I turned around to see Cassidy looking like the portrait of beauty in a signature black dress. I couldn't help but stare. Cassidy's honey brown skin glowed as she flashed a flirtatious smile at me. She wore her long braids in a high donut bun, as her blue feather earrings brushed against her collarbone. Her aura had captured the attention of my senses, both sight and scent, and damn near had me drooling.

I stroked my beard as my mouth tightened slightly. "Damn," I mumbled, soaking her in from head to toe.

"Was it worth the wait?" she inquired.

"Was what worth the wait?"

"Me."

"Oh, most definitely."

She flashed me a grin before turning her back to me. "Thank you. Can you finish zipping me up?"

I looked down to see she was wearing matching bra and panties underneath. My teeth grazed my bottom lips as I pictured her limbs entwined around my waist and my tongue buried between the thighs that were poking out of her dress and begging for my attention. I wanted to lick her down to the bone.

"You sure you don't wanna skip dinner?" I asked, toying with her dress zipper.

She turned her neck in my direction, revealing the canopy of long false lashes covering her eyes. "Hendrix, I can feel you undressing me with my clothes on. Just zip my dress, or we're gonna be late!"

I cinched my arms around her waist as my fingers roamed over her hips. "We already late, so what's the rush now?"

"We're going to be even later!"

"Just let a nigga taste it," I whispered, brushing my lips against her neck.

She quickly darted out of my grasp. "If I miss my best friend's proposal because I was gettin' some dick, she'll never let me live that shit down!"

My eyes zeroed in on her honey-colored face. "You can't get me hooked on somethin' and then take it from me. Especially not lookin' as good as you do right now."

Her cheeks lit up, reddening by the second as she giggled. "As tempting as you are right now, we gotta go! And remember, nobody knows about this you and me shit, and I want to keep it that way!"

"If you think I'm keeping my hands to myself all night, you're wrong," I stated.

She playfully pushed me away. "Hendrix!"

I sucked my teeth. "Aight, fine. You ready?"

She stepped into my space and adjusted the diamond-studded chain around my neck, centering the cross right in the middle of my chest. "There, now it's perfect and now I'm ready."

"Cool, let's go."

I followed behind her, entranced by the way her hips swayed from left to right. Being in the league came with its share of groupies and fake love, but Cassidy was different. She'd always been the realest. I knew how risky long-distance relationships were, but Cassidy was the one risk I was willing to take. I wanted her for the long term.

fourteen

· · ·

CASSIDY

Hendrix was seated to my right at the dinner table set for eight. Donovan had arranged for us to have a private section at the restaurant and a personal chef to cook for all of us. We ate like royalty, stuffing our faces with lobster and roasted sea scallops, and savory creole dishes like conch, goat, and oxtail.

"I'd like to make a toast," Donovan announced, clinking the side of his glass after we'd all let our food digest for a bit.

He stood to his feet as I pulled in a deep breath and held it for a few seconds. It was one of the moments Lauryn had been waiting her whole life for, and I was so happy to be able to share it with her. Donovan was the yin to her yang. They'd been together for the past five years and had seen their shares of ups and downs, but she'd always known he was the one for her.

"I'd just like to thank all of y'all for coming all the way out to this beautiful fuckin' island to celebrate my baby girl's twenty-fifth birthday," he started.

"Yeah, yeah!" Shauna cheered to my left.

"Oweeee!" I purred.

"Yassss!" Brielle cheered.

Donovan then turned his attention to Lauryn who up, until that moment, had no clue what he was about to do. The moment he stepped over to her and got down on one knee, the waterworks began to flow.

"Oh my God!" she screamed, slapping her hand over her cherry-red painted lips.

He took her hand in his. "Baby, I love you. You mean the world to me. Will you make me the happiest man alive and be my wifey?" he asked, before slipping the sparkling diamond ring on her finger.

"Yes! Yes! Oh my fuckin' g—Oh shit! I—I gotta call my mama! I—I gotta call Mark!" she exclaimed.

"Don't worry about that, we got it all right here on live! They saw everything, boo!" Brielle hailed with her phone glued to her hand.

We all cheered virtually alongside her family as Donovan and Lauryn held each other tight and shared a sweet kiss. Once we were done showering the newly engaged couple with two rounds of congratulatory shots, Hendrix leaned over and whispered in my ear, "I'm tired of waiting. I gotta have you right now."

"Here? Hendrix, can we save it for when we get back? I promise you the moment we get through the gate, this pussy is *all yours*," I purred in his ear.

"What I tell you earlier, Cass? Now that I've had you, I'm not gon' quit you. You gon' have to give me more of that right now."

The intimate growl of his voice against my ear made my thighs quiver. To make matters worse, his hand had slipped underneath the table and right up my dress.

I quickly caught his hand, freezing it in place. *Bold ass nigga.* "Yo, chill…" I cautioned.

"Meet me in the bathroom in five minutes or I'ma bend your fine ass over this table, and I don't give a fuck who sees," he warned before exiting the table.

Flustered and feeling challenged, I watched him disappear to the back of the restaurant. I knew better than to call his bluff. He was a sexy, bold ass mothafucka, wasn't no tellin' what he'd do.

"Hey, uh—I'll be right back," I said, angling my body in Shauna's direction.

"Where you goin'?"

"Bathroom," I blurted out.

"You want me to come with you or you good?" she quizzed.

I quickly shook my head. "Nah, I'm good."

Her eyes darted past me, noticing Hendrix's empty seat. "Mmhm. Go on then you lil' nasty." She snickered.

"Shut up!"

Her comment let me know that Hendrix and I weren't as lowkey as we thought we were. Before drawing any more attention to myself, I quickly disappeared to the back of the restaurant where the bathrooms were located. As soon as I approached the men's bathroom, the door opened, and Hendrix pulled me inside and pinned my back against the cold, steel door. I didn't get a word out before his lips mashed against mine. I didn't stop him. I *couldn't*. I was hypnotized by his dominating aura and the strong grip his hands had around the dip of my waist. Of all the feelings circulating through my body, being ready and willing, suddenly made it to the top of the list. His tongue swirled around my mouth until our lips were slathered in saliva.

Pulling my hips forward, I felt his growing dick press against my thigh, begging to be released. I took that as my cue to release the *Kraken* and began fumbling with the Salvatore Ferragamo belt around his waist. We moved our salacious quickie into the closest vacant stall, and I dropped to my knees. Teetering on the four-inch heels and the tips of my toes, I serviced the fuck out of his ass while trying my best not to let my knees touch the floor.

"You so fuckin' nasty, you know that?"

Hendrix's facial expression was set to a handsome scowl as he palmed the top of my bun. He leaned his head back against the door as my lips slid up and down his dick. Nice and sloppy, just the way he liked it.

"Mmm, let me see those pretty ass eyes. I like how you look at me with your mouth wrapped around my dick," he growled.

My eyes glowed with lust as I gently sucked his balls and then ran my tongue up and down the base like I was trying to see how many licks it would take to get to the center of his ten-inch lollipop. Hendrix took turns running his fingers through my braids and cupping the back of my neck.

"Mmm, shit. Come here, girl," he said, letting out a full-throated groan.

He pulled me to my feet and quickly pulled the hem of my dress over my ass and shifted my G-string to the side.

His strong arms quickly had my body suspended in the air as I dug my nails into his firm shoulders.

"Oh fuck," I moaned into his ear, draping my legs around his waist.

Hendrix cupped my breasts and kissed my neck as he instantly fucked me to climax. Even with my hand clasped over my mouth, I could barely stifle out the sound of my moans and screams as he continued to lay the pipe. As soon as we came, he pulled his dripping wet dick out of me and put me down.

"Damn, you squirted all over my shit," he revealed.

My lips curved upward to a smile as I walked over to the sink to wipe down my lady parts and touch up my lipstick. "That's what you get for not being able to keep it in your pants."

"You still owe me when we get back to the spot. I ain't forgot about what you said."

"Oh, I haven't either, but for now we gotta get back out there."

fifteen

. . .

HENDRIX

"Take off your clothes," I demanded the moment we stepped inside the villa.

Cassidy smiled invitingly, peeling her clothes off piece by piece. Completely naked, she jumped into my arms and wrapped her flawless legs around me. The moment we fell across her bed, I rolled on top of her and started planting a trail of kisses from her lips, over to her neck, and back up to her ears while she caressed the tattoos on my back. She thrusted her hips forward and started to fill the room with soft moans. I continued placing kisses on her chest, before sucking and blowing on her rock-hard nipples.

"This pussy still all mine. tonight?" I asked, lowering my lips between her plump hips.

"Yes," she breathed, twitching from the tickle of my beard against her flesh.

"Good, now close your eyes," I commanded.

Her toes instantly curled when I slid two fingers inside her and flicked my tongue against her nipples. "Mmm, shit."

"I just want you to focus on your breathing and focus on how good this shit feels. If you can sync your orgasm to your breathing, you'll cum ten times stronger," I told her.

I massaged her naked body from head to toe, before slowly French kissing her pussy to get it sloppy, dripping wet for me.

"Mmm, fuck," she cursed underneath her breath as I slowly nibbled at the curves of her hips.

"You feel it, Cass?"

Her chin trembled. "M—Mmhm."

"Mmm, cum for daddy," I coached, brushing my tongue up and down her hardened clit.

Cassidy's body quaked underneath my grasp as she came hard and fast, screaming out in pleasure. Before she fully came down from her orgasm, I pushed inside her to send her into another cumming frenzy.

"Oh fuck! Fuck! Fuck! Yessss!" she squealed, spreading her legs wide.

I stroked her body as gently as a violinist as I leaned in to kiss her deeply. She moaned in my mouth as her tight ass walls clung to my dick. I locked my hands underneath her knees and began digging her out until she came again.

"Bring those sexy ass lips over here. I wanna feel them wrapped around my dick again," I announced.

Cassidy crawled in between my legs and onto her knees before taking me into her mouth. I locked my hand around the back of her head before driving my dick to the back of her throat to hear her gag on my shit. With two hands around the base, she quickly grazed her tongue around and across the head.

"Mmm, shit," I groaned as my eyes rolled back in my head. She was a serious head doctor.

My eyes popped open when I felt the warmth of her sweet spot encircle my dick. "Goddamn," I hummed, hands surrounding her petite waist.

The soft skin on her ass rippled when I smacked it as I watched each inch of my dick disappear inside her and reappear as she rode me. My eyes continued downward to her jiggling C-cups before hooking my tongue around her nipple and pulling it into my mouth.

Cassidy sunk her teeth into her bottom lip as her nails sliced up my chest and shoulder blades. "Mmm, shit. You're gonna make me cum again," she confessed.

"That's my job," I mumbled before placing kisses in the crevice between her shoulder and neck.

Switching positions, I flipped her over on all fours and started eating her ass from the back. My tongue skated up the arch in her back before I licked my fingers and pushed one inside her tight ass. Her body shivered with desire as I finger-fucked her ass with one hand and her pussy with the other.

I slipped underneath her body and pulled her down to ride my face so I could write love letters to her pussy with my tongue.

"Oooh fuckkkkkkkk!" she squealed, squirting her pussy juices into my mouth and all through my beard.

I ran my hand down my mouth and licked my fingers before mounting her from behind. Her shit was good to the last drop. I hooked my arm around her waist and gripped her thigh as I slow stroked her from behind. She threw it back, making sure I hit her spot with each stroke.

"Mmm, shit. You got a nigga wantin' to go balls deep in that fuckin' pussy."

"Do it. Give me every inch," she demanded.

My body hovered over hers as I pushed her head down into the bed and gave her what she asked for. With her arms folded and pressed behind her back, her squeals and moans echoed throughout the room.

I pulled out and spit in her sweet ass pussy, licking her to her next climax. My eyes flashed up at hers from in between her thighs. She longed for sleep, but her creaming pussy told me she wanted more. Soon, my tongue was coated with another round of her love juices.

"Shit!" she exclaimed, panting violently until her breaths settled into a yawn.

"Mmm, you tappin' out?" I asked.

Cassidy slowly shook her head. "No. I'm not," she purred.

"Good, because I'ma fuck you to sleep and then I'm gon' wake you up with the dick."

sixteen

. . .

Day Seven

CASSIDY

On our last day on the island, I woke up to the sweet feeling of Hendrix's face buried in between my thighs.

"Hendrix, stop it! What are you doing?" I giggled, knowing I wanted to pee and at least brush my teeth before we started up again. He'd been wearing my ass out over the past few days, and as tired as I was, I wasn't going to turn down the D.

"Check out ain't til' noon, so I'm finna lick, suck, and fuck you til they throw us out this mothafucka," he preached.

"Can I at least go to the bathroom first?"

He smirked. "Go ahead, but you already know what time it is when you get back."

"Yeah, okay," I said before prancing my naked body across the floor and closing the bathroom door behind me.

After flushing, I stood in front of the sink lathering my hands with soap and running them underneath the warm water. While staring back at my reflection in the mirror, I started to think about the hell of a week I'd shared with Hendrix. If anyone had asked me what I thought would happen on the island, finding solace in Hendrix Croft wouldn't have been one of them. Yet, I'd never felt more fulfilled—physically and emotionally. Before I could reach out to turn off the faucet, Hendrix tapped on the door.

"Yeah?" I asked, shaking my hands dry.

"You good?"

I opened the door and lifted my eyes to his. One look at me, and I became transparent, baring more to him than a hairless pussy and a set of hard nipples. His eyes were filled with compassion coated in desire.

I cleared my throat. "Y—yeah."

"Where'd you go just now?" he asked, swiping a few tousled braids behind my ear.

"Nowhere, I'm here. I'm good."

"You sure?"

I forced a bright smile in his direction before making my way back over to the bed. "Yeah, I'm good. I promise."

Even a blind man could see I was lying. Something had a hold on me, and he was six-foot-four and still had my love juices glistening across his face.

"So what happens now?" he asked, cuddling up beside me on the bed.

"I thought I was supposed to be gettin' fucked and sucked until they threw us out of here," I joked, mocking him.

He chuckled. "Nah, I mean between you and me when we leave here."

My brows sloped as I sat up on my elbows. "What do you mean?"

"Contrary to what you think, you're not just another notch in my belt, Cassidy. Fate brought us here. That shit brought us back together after all this time, tell me you don't feel it too."

I huffed. Hendrix did more than fulfill my body sexually, he fed my soul. He was a goddamn hazard to my health. I was prepared for our secret to stay between the sheets in St. Martin, but he was on some other shit.

"I just don't get where all this is coming from. Like, why me? Why now?"

"I've had my eye on you since we were fuckin' kids, Cass. But you were the only female who never gave me the time of day. You didn't give a fuck about my money, what my father did, or nothin'. Everybody around me was lookin' to ride my coattails for a come up, and only a handful of niggas stayed down, family included. You're the realest girl I've ever met, and I'm not letting you get away again."

He sighed after letting those words fly out of his mouth and into the universe. His confession had left my thoughts in limbo. *Let me get away again?* When had I ever been his? Clearly, he wasn't thinking straight.

"Hendrix, you were in Vegas and now you're going thousands of miles away to play in Kansas City. I'm in San Jose. I'm sorry, but we both know it—it would never work."

"That's why we have access to airplanes, Cassidy. And then there's the off season. Next," he said, shooting down my best excuse.

Fuck, this nigga's not taking no for an answer, I thought to myself. *He's not serious. He can't be serious. There's no way he's serious, right?* My anxieties and insecurities swarmed around my mind like a hive of angry bees. We were far from the shallow end and seconds away from falling all the way in love.

"Tell me what you scared of."

The genuine tone of his voice set fire to my core. One thing I'd never been afraid of was love. I was a lover of love, so much that it had been easy for me to become love drunk over a nigga, especially in my younger days. I just couldn't stand anymore embarrassment. If I gave into Hendrix and he played me out, I didn't think I could live it down.

"I just don't want this to be a rebound thing for me or an *only when you're lonely* thing for you," I admitted.

"A rebound is irrelevant if I was here first, and I ain't never had a problem being lonely, Cass."

I kissed my teeth. "You know what I mean, Hendrix. I came here to get over a man, not find a whole new one!"

"That nigga wasn't a man, and we both know it. I would never do no sucka shit like that to you. That's not in my blood and you know it."

"Hendrix, can we please just—"

"Listen, we can take this shit as slow or as fast as you want. I'll give you time to heal, and when you're ready just know I'm next up. I don't have a problem sitting in the passenger seat if you're the one driving, Cass."

His words melted the cold, steel wall around my heart one syllable at a time. "This is crazy! This is absolute madness, Hendrix! We can't be doing this, can we?" I asked, before burying my head in the palms of my hands.

Millions of thoughts raced through my computerized mind. Half the time I wasn't sure what I wanted, so when I did make a commitment that meant I was serious about it, and I didn't know if I could say the same for him. This was no longer just sex. Hendrix was talking about learning each other with hundreds if not thousands of miles between us. I enjoyed quality time and just because he checked off many of my boxes, I didn't know if I could handle the distance. Of all the things I was unsure about, he wasn't one of them. Truth be told, *I just wasn't ready to let go.*

Before responding, he cradled me in between his muscular arms and kissed the top of my head. "As far as I'm concerned, you've always been mine," he whispered.

The End

afterword

Reader,

Thank you for reading Cassidy and Hendrix's love story. Please, if you've made it this far, I hope you'll consider taking a minute to tell me what you thought about the book in the form of a **book review and/or rating**. Don't hesitate to let me know what you'd like to see from me next! I thoroughly enjoy reading your reviews and hearing from you as well! I'm always striving to attract new readers and retain current ones, and reviews are one of the easiest ways to attract readers. If you loved the book, tell a friend, and most importantly let me know!

All my love,

K.L. Hall

about the author

As a serial storyteller, K.L. Hall pens enthralling love stories intertwined with the grittiness of urban fiction. Her writing style is a fusion of eminently relatable female characters like Sydney Tate and Raquel Valentine, and the flawed, yet desirable male leads who love them, like Law Calloway and Justice Silva.

Sign up for my mailing list to stay up to date with new releases, giveaways, sneak peeks, and more! https://www.authorklhall.com

also by k.l. hall

Diary of a Hood Princess 1-3

Rise of a Street King: The Justice Silva Story *(Spin-Off to the Diary of a Hood Princess series)*

Where He Belongs: A Disrespectful Love Story

Love Me Harder: A Sin City Love Story

Broken Condoms and Promises 1-3

In the Arms of a Savage 1-3

Built for a Savage: Blaze and Camille's Love Story *(Spin-Off to the In the Arms of a Savage Series)*

A Ruthle$$ Love Story 1-3

Fallin' for the Alpha of the Streets 1-2

The Most Savage of Them All: The Wolfe Calloway Story *(Prequel to the In the Arms of a Savage Series)*

When a Gangsta Loves a Good Girl

Caught Between my Husband and a Hustler

The Illest Taboo 1-2

To the Only Thug I'll Ever Love

Novellas:

Bi-Curious: An Erotic Tale

Bi-Curious 2: Tastes Like Candy

House of Cards 1-2

A Savage Calloway Christmas *(Christmas novella to the In the Arms of a Savage Series)*

Lovin' the Alpha of the Streets: A Valentine's Day Novella *(Valentine's Day novella to the Fallin' for the Alpha of the Streets Series)*

Awakened: A Paranormal Romance

As Long as You Stay Down

Solace in Seven

Children's Books:

Princess for Hire

Princess Twinkle Toes & the Missing Magic Sneakers

Little One, Change the World

Adjust Your Crown: A Self-Love Coloring Book for Children of Color

Non-Fiction:

Authors are a Business: The Booked & Busy Course Mini Book

www.ingramcontent.com/pod-product-compliance
Lightning Source LLC
Chambersburg PA
CBHW071233170626
46809CB00008BA/3038